TO LOVE AGAIN

It is 1945 and the lives of families have changed. The pain and memories of the war years have left their mark. Lizzie Vale, the carefree girl — once an aspiring journalist — has changed and become a dedicated nurse. She fights to help her patients recover from their terrible injuries and falls in love with Daniel Miles. Could they ever have a future? Injuries and family prejudice present seemingly insuperable obstacles, but Lizzie is a force to be reckoned with.

CHRISSIE LOVEDAY

TO LOVE AGAIN

Complete and Unabridged

LINFORD
Leicester

First published in Great Britain in 2012

First Linford Edition
published 2013

British Library CIP Data

Loveday, Chrissie.
  To love again. - -
  (Linford romance library)
  1. Love stories.
  2. Large type books.
  I. Title II. Series
  823.9'2–dc23

  ISBN 978–1–4448–1470–5

Published by
F. A. Thorpe (Publishing)
Anstey, Leicestershire

Set by Words & Graphics Ltd.
Anstey, Leicestershire
Printed and bound in Great Britain by
T. J. International Ltd., Padstow, Cornwall

This book is printed on acid-free paper

1945

Cobridge House was silent. Jenny, the nearest thing to a servant still living there, was busily preparing some sort of evening meal. Gone were the days of three maids, a cook, a housekeeper and several others who came in part-time to do various jobs. The unused rooms were sheeted down and apart from having the windows opened once a week, lay damp and dusty. Her little boy cried out.

'All right, Tom, I'm coming,' she called. 'You might have stayed asleep for another half hour,' she muttered softly. Another half hour and she would have been ready for Nellie's return from work.

She did what she could but it was a very large place to keep going single handed. The three-year-old was bouncing in his cot, now somewhat too small for him but at least it meant he was safe when she put him down for his rest. She would have to ask Nellie if she could move him into a bed soon. There were enough of them, after all.

She brought the boy down to the warm kitchen and sat him on the floor with a couple of baking tins and wooden spoons to play with. She heard the front door open and looked to see who was there. It was Nellie, the mistress of the house.

'Jenny, have you heard the news? The war's over! I can't believe it. After all these years, it's finally over. We can all get back to normal. Isn't it wonderful?'

'Yes, ma'm. Wonderful, I'm sure.' Tears brimmed in her eyes.

'Oh, Jenny, how thoughtless of me.' She reached out to the young widow and gave her a hug. 'Poor Ben won't be coming back when the other men return. I've grieved for my brother, of course, but never as much as you must have done. But little Tom is the image of his Daddy. It's a blessing we have him with us.'

'Thank you, Mrs . . . Nellie. It's hard to think he's gone, wiped out just like that. He was always so alive, if you know what I mean. I don't think I shall ever forget that day when the telegram arrived: *Missing believed killed in action*.' Nellie saw the ever-ready tears in the girl's eyes and stretched out her hand again.

'So hard for you.' She sighed. 'Two years ago. Mum didn't get over his loss, either.'

'She'd been bad for a while, though, hadn't she?'

'True, but I think that was the last straw for her. Losing a son is a dreadful thing. Sad times and all the more poignant now it's all over.' Jenny wiped her eyes and took a deep breath to calm herself.

'But, I'm not the only one. There'll be plenty just like me, lost their husbands and fathers and brothers. It's a great relief to know it's all over, though, isn't it? I wonder how long it will take any of us to get back to what things once were?'

'I doubt anything will be quite the same ever again. There's any number of potbanks closed down that will never get going again. We were one of the lucky ones, getting contracts from the Government to make stuff for hospitals and such. Our fine bone china will soon be made again but, thankfully, the earthenware has kept us going.'

'Be nice to see pretty things back in the shops.'

'I suspect that won't be for some time yet. Plain white or cream is still the order of the day. We were allowed to add bands of colour for a couple of years but even that was considered frivolous and too expensive. Ah, well. Now, did you manage to find something for our dinner this evening?'

'Just vegetables, I'm afraid. Turnips and mashed potatoes and I've made some gravy from the stock we kept back.'

'Well done. Mr James isn't going to be best pleased but he really isn't aware of the problems we have.'

Nellie's husband was often complaining about the short rations, even though he had the lion's share of everything that came into the house. The owner of Cobridge's Fine Bone China, James had never been used to any sort of deprivation before this war. He expected things to remain as they had always been. Poor Jenny did her limited best. She had stayed living with the family because she had nowhere else to go.

Once the nursemaid to their son, William, now a strapping fifteen-year-old and away at school, she had moved back to live with them when Ben joined the Army. The other servants were long gone to employment in the war effort or the services.

'Your Joe'll be pleased now it's over, won't he? He might get some proper help back on the farm.' Nellie's other brother, Joe, lived with his in-laws on a farm near Barlaston and was now running it with only the help of his wife, Daisy, and a land girl, who was worse than useless.

'I don't think they've done too badly. They've even let us have a few extras when they could. Luckily, Daisy had been brought up to help in the dairy, so they could manage.'

'Their little 'un must be growing up. What is she? Five, near enough?'

'That's right. Sally goes to school next term. Doesn't seem possible, does it? How the years go by. I'd better go and change now before James gets home. Then I need to write some letters. I haven't heard a thing from Lizzie in ages.'

Jenny nodded and got back to her chores. She thought about Nellie's youngest sibling. Lizzie had always been such a livewire about the place. In fact, if it hadn't been for Lizzie, she doubted she would ever have married her lovely Ben.

Lizzie had taken all sorts of risks to

get them together, even to the point of serving dinner to guests on one occasion, so she could go out with Ben. She smiled at the memory. They'd all been totally gobsmacked when Lizzie had given up her job with Nellie and gone off to be a nurse. Of all people, Lizzie being a nurse was the most unlikely. She was so independent and such a rebel, it was amazing that she'd stuck at it for so long. Over two years now, but from what she had said, it hadn't been easy.

She was always in trouble with the matron for something or other. Even though Jenny had been a nursemaid, she knew she could never have coped in a hospital, especially with the wounded soldiers coming in all the time. Maybe now the war was over, Lizzie would come back home as well and things would soon get better. A bit of life back in this house was what they needed.

Nellie sat by her dressing table. It ought to be an evening of celebration and not a dull meal of mashed turnip and tatties. Perhaps a bottle of wine from the now depleted cellar would help.

It depended on James's mood when he came in. He'd been morose for many months now and it was getting them all down. Granted, times were hard and he had many responsibilities but they needed to look with new life at the future prospects. She looked forward to getting back to what she did best . . . designing the pottery and organising the work in the decorating shop at the factory.

For years now, she had been just a manager, needed only to help keep the girls motivated and work progressing. She was bored by the restrictions. There was never enough clay and often a shortage of coal to fuel the huge bottle ovens. It was frustrating and very annoying. She had managed to obtain supplies simply by the force of her own personality but this was never what she wanted to do.

She looked at her reflection and took out one of her nicest necklaces. It might cheer her up. Heavens, she was getting old. Thirty-eight next birthday and several grey hairs and at least three extra wrinkles. Not that James seemed to have noticed. He was far too pre-occupied these days. She brushed her hair and went downstairs to the dining room where her writing desk now lived.

Dear Lizzie, she began. I hope you are well. Now we have finally received the wonderful news we've been waiting for so long, I'm hoping you will soon return home to us. The factory will soon be working normally I'm sure, and I shall need your help. Perhaps we can even find time to work on those books for children we talked about so long ago. I haven't heard any of your news for such a long time. Try to find time to write when you can. Your ever loving sister, Nellie.

Nellie never found writing easy. She had left school as soon as she could to help keep the family together. It had been desperate at times, when her father had been injured down the coal mines and her mother had been ill.

Her meagre earnings had barely kept food on the table. But, a lot of luck and her own talents had helped her get noticed by the factory owner's son. Not that everything had been easy over the years. She laughed as she remembered becoming mistress of the house where she had been a servant for some years. The others had never known quite what to call her.

Having been *Nellie* to them, they couldn't manage to call her Madam and eventually reverted to *Mrs Nellie*. James was more concerned than she was, but she had soon grown into her role and controlled her staff well. Poor Jenny had taken on so many responsibilities for them that she never had the chance to live her own life any more.

The phone rang and Nellie went to answer it.

'Nellie?' Lizzie's excited voice rang out. 'Isn't it just terrific news? I had to call you and well, just rejoice that it's all over.'

'Lizzie, lovely to hear you. How strange. I've just been writing to you to ask how you are. We haven't heard from you for such a long time.'

'I know. It's been frantic here. And no doubt it will be for some months. There are people coming home with terrible injuries and I'm needed.'

'Oh, I see. I was hoping you'd come home soon and help us get back to normal.'

'Not for a while yet, I'm afraid. I have finally got matron to accept that it doesn't matter if I arrive at work with my cloak fastened the wrong way. The patients all love me as I am and I can make them laugh a bit.'

Nellie listened as her little sister prattled on. She could fully believe that her patients loved her bright pretty face and lively smile. The battles she had at first with the matron seemed to have faded.

'So, is it all right if I come over for the weekend?'

'I'm sorry. Yes, of course it will be fine. This weekend?'

'Yes, of course. You see, I really need to see poor old Charlie. I have to tell him finally that I can't marry him.'

'Oh, poor Charlie. He'll be devastated. Are you quite sure about this? After all, you've been engaged to him for over five years.'

'Yes, and we're no nearer getting married. Surely that must tell you something?'

'We'll talk about it at the weekend. Will you come Friday night?'

'Of course I will. I'll let you know what time. Must dash now. Bye, darling Nellie. Terrific news.' She hung up and Nellie took a deep breath. Lizzie always had that effect on people. An absolute dynamo, always so full of life.

'Jenny! That was Lizzie,' she called as she went through to the kitchen. 'She's coming home at the weekend. We'll need to air her room and get the bed ready.'

'That's lovely. It will make things seem more normal, won't it? More like old times when she was living here.'

'It's only a weekend visit, but it's better than nothing. She wants to see Charlie, so he may be joining us for tea on Sunday. Wouldn't be surprised if Joe and Daisy came over as well. Though what we shall find to feed them on, I'm not sure. I expect it will be weeks before rationing ends. We'll have a go at making one of those special recipe cakes. There's one that's egg-less. Have we got some dried fruit left?'

'I think there's a bit, kept back.'

'I'll look up the recipe in a minute and we'll try it out on Saturday. We'll need margarine, too, but that shouldn't be a problem.'

'There's a tin of best salmon put by

as well. We've been saving it for a special occasion.'

'That must be pretty old. At least four or five years. I hope it's still safe to use.'

'Course it is. It's in a tin. I can make a fresh loaf and we'll soon have a feast fit for everyone.'

'Well done, Jenny. You're a marvel. I'll phone Joe anyway and see if they can come. Pity William can't have the weekend off school and come home too. Make it a real celebration.'

'There's Mr James coming in now, I think.'

Nellie went into the hall and helped her husband out of his coat.

'Great news, isn't it, love?' she said.

'Fantastic. I thought we might celebrate. Go out for supper?'

'Jenny's made something for us, but it's a nice idea. I thought we might open a bottle of wine? She can join us for the evening. It's going to be difficult for her with the servicemen all coming home and her having lost our Ben.'

'Fine. We'll go out another time. You look nice,' he said as he fingered her diamond necklace. 'I haven't seen you wearing this for a while.'

'I wanted to make a bit of an effort. Oh, and Lizzie telephoned. She's got leave at the weekend so she's coming home. I thought I'd telephone Joe and Daisy, too, so we can have a little family party.'

'Why not. If you can find anything to feed them. We seem to have been on short rations for ever. I'll see what I can find in the way of wine. Oh, I did hear the men talking about a bonfire they're setting up in the park. The band will be out there and there's even mention of some rockets left over from before the war. I thought we might stroll down there later on.'

'How exciting. Shall we take Jenny and Tom as well? It might cheer her up.'

'I suppose so. It's difficult with her, isn't it? She's a servant but a sort of ex-family member.'

'Nothing ex-family about her. She's

our sister-in-law. She manages the house very well on her own, considering we used to have I don't know how many women working for us. Not to mention a full-time gardener and other people who came in.'

'We'll soon have things back to normal. The boy who comes in to help in the garden has done reasonably well. Kept us going with some extra vegetables. We'll get someone more capable when they are available. Get a new housekeeper and a few maids, too. And a cook, of course. Someone properly qualified.'

'It would be nice but it may be harder than you think. Women have had a taste of being more independent. They may not want come back to the sort of work we'd be offering.'

★ ★ ★

James frowned slightly at his meal but made no comment. Jenny sat with them looking slightly awkward. She had a small amount of wine in her glass and sipped it as if it was poison. Tom had been put to bed as usual but the plan was to wake him later to take him to join the celebrations.

When the main course was finished, Jenny brought in a junket, made from powdered milk for dessert.

'I used to love this when I was little,' James said bravely. Nellie grimaced. It had never been a thing she liked, but she hadn't the heart to tell Jenny so she smiled and bravely ate her portion without comment.

At nine o'clock, the sleepy little boy was lifted from his cot and outdoor clothes put on over his pyjamas. Jenny put him in the old pushchair that had been kept from when William was a toddler and the little group set off for the park.

Clearly the word had spread and everyone was talking and laughing excitedly. The area of the park usually kept for football was filled with people. A massive bonfire had been put together very quickly and the band, largely consisting of the young people and one or two old stagers, made a lively noise, cheerful rather than musical, but nobody minded.

Flags were waved and small groups of cheering began to resound everywhere. Nellie found herself moved to tears. Partly joy that it was over and partly sadness for all the families who had lost loved ones. She gripped Jenny's hand and they shared the moment, each thinking of the one special man who would never return.

A bright but rather erratic rocket shot up through the now darkening sky and a massive cheer arose. Several of the smaller children began to cry at the sudden noise. Little Tom stared, not certain whether to laugh or cry.

'That was exciting, wasn't it?' James said to the child. Tom looked unconvinced but gave a feeble smile. 'I think there's going to be another one. Ready? Watch over there.'

A second rocket took off, even more

erratic than the first and landed close to the bonfire. 'I think they may have lost something over the years,' James laughed. Nellie caught his hand happily. She hadn't seen him so relaxed in many months and it delighted her to catch a glimpse of the old James she had fallen in love with.

Wearily, they reached home well after eleven o'clock after joining with the spontaneous dancing. Though extremely tired, sleep was not easy and she and James lay awake for some hours. Planning the future was once more a possibility after so many years of living with the war.

At least his work had been acknowledged as a reserved occupation and had allowed him to stay at home and not be a part of the fighting forces. For that, she would be ever grateful.

Lizzie arrived home late on Friday afternoon. She rushed into the kitchen to see her friend, Jenny, and little Tom.

'My, who's this great big boy? What have you done with little Tom?' she asked, laughing, pretending to look under the table.

'I'm Tom. Me. I've growed,' he announced. 'Hello, Lizzie. Why have you got a funny coat?'

'It's my nurse's cloak. Jenny, however are you managing? I hope my sister isn't working you too hard. You look exhausted.'

'It is hard work but then we all have to do our bit, don't we? Nellie and Mr James have been very good to me so it's the least I can do. Nellie is always working hard herself so I'm pleased to be able to do what I can for them.'

'That's good of you. So, what's new here?'

'Nowt much.' She went on to tell her about the exciting evening in the park with the bonfire, which was just about the only thing she could think of.

'I've been busy, of course. So many poor men coming back with horrific injuries. One does what's possible but I sometimes think it isn't enough. At least I've now reached a decision about

Charlie Swift. I know I can never marry him. If I could, I would have done it long ago. We've grown apart now.'

'That won't be easy.'

'I know. I'm dreading it. I need to phone and tell him I want to see him tomorrow afternoon. I might leave it till tomorrow morning. Oh, is that our Nellie coming in?' Without waiting for an answer she whirled round and went into the hall. 'Nellie. Darling Nellie. How are you? You look as worn out as Jenny there.'

'I'm fine, thank you very much. It's so lovely to see you. You're looking well but you're thinner than ever.'

'It's hard work being a nurse. Rushed off my feet most of the time, I am.'

'I'll ask Jenny to make us some tea and we'll go and sit down and you can tell me all your news.'

Saying Goodbye To Charlie

It was a cheerful evening, buoyed with the anticipation of a peaceful future. After so many years of war, everyone wanted to get back to the way things were before.

'I think I've changed a bit too much to go back to the way things were,' Lizzie announced. 'This is why I have to finish things with Charlie. I know it's the right thing to do but I know he'll be very hurt.'

'He always talks about you when I see him,' James told her. 'He's still doing our printing and I shall want to keep him on. I hope that won't be a problem?'

'I hope not. He's a good bloke but he's not right for me. I'll call him in the morning and hopefully see him tomorrow afternoon. Wish me luck.'

'Is there someone else?' Nellie asked,

suddenly realising the possibility.

'Of course not, I wouldn't cheat on him. Even after all these years. What do you take me for?'

'Sorry. It was just a thought.' Despite her words, Lizzie was blushing slightly but wisely, Nellie did not pursue it. 'I thought I'd invite Joe and Daisy and little Sally to come for tea on Sunday. Daisy's dad is quite capable of doing the milking for once.'

'Good. That might mean they'll bring some goodies with them. Haven't had any proper cream for ages and I do hate that evaporated milk we're supposed to think is cream. Goodness me, all these old married couples with children. I'm really on the shelf, aren't I?'

'Your own choice, Lizzie, isn't it?' James said wisely.

'Touché, brother dear. But I'd probably have been married to Charlie's parents more than him. Right miserable pair they are. His mother never speaks and his father just grumbles. Surprising that Charlie is actually as nice as he is.'

'Sounds as if you're regretting your decision already,' he said.

'Not at all. I just need to be fair to him. Right, well I'm off to bed. I can actually have a whole night's sleep without fear of being called in to work or sheltering from the bombs.'

'Oh my dear, is it really that bad?' Nellie asked in distress.

'Just sometimes. I have to go in if there's a sudden influx of patients. But not tonight. I shall sleep in peace in a wonderful, comfy bed. Nighty-night both of you. Sleep well.' She bounced off and slammed the door as she went.

'I never imagined our little Lizzie would ever be such a dedicated nurse,' Nellie said with a smile.

'I suspect there is someone special, you know. Did you see how she blushed when I asked her?'

'Maybe you're right. Now, how about an early night for us as well? I've got that exhausted Friday feeling.'

'If you like. I have to go in to work in

the morning, of course, but should be home by lunchtime.'

'I'm trying out that wonderful egg-less cake in the morning. Should be interesting!'

'I'm not sure cooking is your strongest point, my dear. But good luck. I'll be up in a minute or two.'

Wartime rations meant that breakfast at Cobridge House was a very simple affair. Gone were the days of a selection of cooked dishes lined up on the sideboard. Now, it was mostly taken in the kitchen and consisted of tea and toast. James hated it and often asked for a tray in his dressing room.

His newspaper was no longer delivered and he was forced to collect it on his way to the factory. Jenny and Nellie usually took the chance to talk about the day's arrangements and list the various chores that needed doing. This Saturday, everything was different. With Lizzie's presence there was an air of jollity about the place, even if tempered slightly by the coming break-up with

Charlie. James put his head round the door and announced he was leaving for work.

'I hope things go as planned for you all. I'll see you at lunchtime.'

'Bye, James,' Lizzie called. The other two called their goodbyes and settled back to discussing the recipe for the cake.

'We need fourteen ounces of dried fruit. It can be anything we can find mixed together. Four ounces of margarine and then some of the sugar is substituted with saccharine tablets.'

'Yum,' Lizzie said with heavy sarcasm. 'Come back, Mrs Brownlow, all is forgiven.' Mrs Brownlow had been their cook for many years and something of a wonder she'd been. 'Wonder what she's doing with herself these days.'

'No point having a proper cook until rationing looks like ending. I shall look for someone to do a bit more in the garden as soon as possible. Now, Lizzie, not wishing to hurry you, but hadn't you better make this telephone call of yours? Get it over with.'

With a sigh, Lizzie went into the hall and sat by the phone, staring at it as if it could tell her something. She picked up the handset and waited for the operator to reply.

'Longton, four-three-seven, please.' She gave the home number and waited as the rings sounded.

'Hello? Swift Printing. Charlie Swift speaking.'

Lizzie's heart thumped and she nearly put the phone down again. She drew in her breath again and slightly hesitant, she spoke.

'Charlie? Hello, it's me. Lizzie.'

'Lizzie, my dear. How are you? It's ages since we spoke. Where are you?'

'I'm fine, thank you. I'm staying with Nellie and James. Just for the weekend. I was wondering if we might meet this afternoon, if you're free.'

'For you, of course I am. Oh, it's so good to hear your voice. What time and where shall I meet you? Or shall I come to your sister's house? You could come here, of course, but you know how things are. Actually, saying that, I do have some news on that score. I'll tell you everything this afternoon.'

'How about we meet at the pavilion in the park? We can have tea. For old times' sake.'

'That sounds great. Oh, Lizzie, I have missed you. I'll see you later. Three o'clock. And don't be late. Wonderful. Bye now.'

'Goodbye, Charlie.' With a heavy heart, she replaced the phone and sat awhile staring at it. He sounded so happy to hear from her. He was going to be devastated when she told him it was all off.

'Is everything all right, love?' Nellie asked as she came into the hall.

'I suppose so. Oh, Nellie, he sounded so pleased to hear from me and now I'm going to spoil everything for him. But I am doing the right thing, aren't I?'

'If you feel you don't love him any

more, then of course you are. But are you sure you really want to finish with him? You've been engaged for such a long time. It might just be that everything's gone stale because nothing is happening.'

'No. I'm sure it's over. I know we haven't been seeing each other very much, but neither of us are the same young people we used to be. I had no experience of anything other than here and home when we got engaged. He was my first boyfriend, wasn't he?'

'James was mine.'

'Yes, but that was different. You did so many things. Lots of jobs and then you married the boss of everything.'

'We didn't have it easy at the time. Remember James's father cut us off completely. We had to find lodgings and he was forced to move out of Cobridge House altogether. Anyway, that doesn't help. You know what you want to do. If you don't love him, then there's no way you should get married. Good luck. I'm going to phone Joe and Daisy now.

They should be about finished with milking.'

'What do you think I should wear this afternoon?' Lizzie asked.

'For goodness' sake. You never change, do you? Help yourself to anything you want in my wardrobe if you've nothing of your own.'

'Thanks, Nellie.' She raced upstairs as if her date was within the next few minutes. Nellie shook her head and telephoned her brother.

They would like to come the next day, according to his wife, Daisy, but they would have to catch the bus as they had no petrol coupons left. It was too far for Sally to come in the pony and trap so it would be a short visit.

It seemed to Nellie that even if the war was over, it was going to take a very long time before it made a proper difference to the lives of everyone. At least they knew it was safe to lie in their beds at night without fear of the sirens going off. It hadn't affected them greatly, but there had been several bombs dropped around the area.

Often they were discharged when the planes were on their way home, so one could never be certain. They had taken to sleeping downstairs when the sirens sounded, rather than go to the shelter in the garden.

'I didn't bring a coat home with me,' Lizzie said as she came down the stairs. 'I didn't think I'd need it. It is May, after all, but can I borrow this jacket?'

'Course you can. What will you wear with it?'

'Can I borrow this skirt as well. Oh, and that nice blouse of yours?'

* * *

Nellie made her cake while Jenny baked bread. The kitchen smelled wonderful and they were all ready for lunch when the time came.

They had vegetable soup and fresh bread. The ever-simmering pot on the side of the stove kept them in savoury stock and all bones and scraps were added to it to make soups and sauces. Lizzie had become quiet as the time approached for her meeting with Charlie.

'You are quite certain this is what you want?' Nellie asked as her sister changed into her selected outfit for the event.

'It's the only fair thing to do. I've kept him waiting long enough.'

Nellie watched as her little sister, quite the young lady now, set off along the road. At least it was a nice sunny day.

★　★　★

Lizzie stood by the lake, watching the young people playing around on the boats.

'Hello, you,' said a voice behind her, and a pair of arms reached round her waist.

'Charlie. Hello to you, too.' She turned to face him and he leaned over to kiss her. She pulled back and he kissed the air between them. 'Too many people around,' she said feebly. 'Shall we go in for tea?'

'You look gorgeous. More new clothes?'

'Nellie's, of course. I don't have any coupons left and I didn't bring much home with me.' She moved away from him and stood very still.

'What's wrong, Lizzie? It's weeks since we saw each other. I thought you would be pleased to see me. You haven't even written to me for ages.'

'I know. Nellie said the same thing. It's been terribly busy at the hospital. You have no idea how long we have to work every day. By the time I get back to the nurses' hostel, I am so exhausted, I just want to sleep.'

'I know. You've been having a difficult time. It must be terrible to see such injuries.'

'Yes. But it has to be done. Charlie . . . I . . . '

'Let's find a table and order some tea. I heard a rumour that they still

33

have cakes for sale. I'll go and get something and you can sit quietly and wait for me.'

She sat at a corner table, a quiet spot where she hoped they could talk. Somehow, it seemed right to be here, the place where they had spent so many Sundays in their early days. She hoped, too, that being in public would stop them having an unpleasant scene.

'Here we go. Pot of tea for two and cream cakes. I suspect it isn't really cream, but it's the best they can do.'

'Amazing they can produce anything at all really. Thank you. It looks lovely.'

'So, how are things really with you? Any signs of you leaving nursing and coming back to the factory? And your writing, of course. Are you planning any more articles?'

'I haven't had time to consider it.' Lizzie had been a regular contributor to the Staffordshire Evening Post, the local paper. Though she had originally hoped to be a journalist, she had begun to enjoy being a personal assistant to her sister at Cobridge's. She had fulfilled her writing ambitions by producing occasional articles for the Editor. 'And I shall stay on in nursing for some months yet.' Charlie looked crestfallen.

'I was hoping we could plan for our wedding before too long. I know that my parents have always been something of a blight on the landscape, but I have some news on that score.'

'Charlie,' Lizzie tried to interrupt, but he was not listening.

'At last they have agreed to move out of the flat. My mother is sick of not being able to go out, and they have got a council flat. Ground floor, of course. So we shall have our own place, all to ourselves and you'll be able to decorate it just as you like. We can get new furniture as my parents will want to take most things with them. So, what do you say to that?'

Lizzie busied herself pouring tea and passing the cup. She tried to avoid his gaze and was still wondering why her usual ability to find the right words seemed to have deserted her altogether.

'It sounds good for you. Space and time for yourself at last. But Charlie, I'm sorry but . . . '

'But you don't want to live above the shop. I suppose I should have known that after you've lived at Cobridge House for so long. Our flat hardly compares to the luxury you have there. But we can make it cosy. It's not too far from your sister's factory and until we have a family, you'll still be able to work. Though I hope it won't be too long before we can start a family.'

'Charlie . . . there isn't going to be any wedding or any family. Not for you and I. I am so sorry but I can't marry you.'

He looked suddenly angry. His eyes narrowed and his usual smile turned into a hard line.

'And is there an explanation for this change of heart? We've been engaged for more than five years. We'd have been married years ago if it hadn't been for this war.'

'There were too many other reasons as well. I think I realised some time ago that we never rushed to get married because it wasn't the right thing to do.'

'So why now?' Charlie's voice shook with anger.

'I don't know. I just felt it was time to call a halt.'

'So, who is he? Who's taken over my place in your affections?'

'Nobody,' she whispered miserably. Her eyes filled with tears. 'I have never been unfaithful to you. I wouldn't do that.'

'So why, Lizzie? I've been loyal to you. I have never looked at anyone else and not because I haven't had opportunities. I love you and always have done.'

'I loved you, too, Charlie, but I've changed. I've seen so many things in recent years. Things that have changed me. I'm not sure what I want any more.'

'But it clearly isn't me. I have to go.'

'But you haven't had your tea.'

'How can I drink tea? Or eat cakes.

Why did you have to choose this place to tell me? Of all places, this is the one that will always remind me of you. I'm going.'

He got up and stormed out, leaving her sitting in the corner with a tray of tea and cakes. This encounter had been worse than she could have imagined.

She burst into tears and rushed out of the café. Not yet ready to face anyone, she walked round the park.

Lizzie eventually turned for home and walked slowly back to her family. She wiped her eyes and hoped she didn't look too much of a wreck. The engagement ring weighed heavily in her pocket and she knew it would have to be returned. Poor Charlie. She should have finished this years ago. But being away from home, it had seemed remote and unreal.

'Are you all right?' Nellie asked. She was waiting anxiously in the hall. 'Only you've been ages. I expected you back much earlier. How did it go?'

'It was worse than I expected. At first

he just looked hurt and shocked and then he got angry. I went for a walk afterwards but it didn't help. Oh Nellie, I feel terrible about it. And I forgot to give him the ring back. It's still in my pocket. I can't see him again so I suppose I'd better send it.'

'I'll see he gets it back. Don't worry.'

A Face From The Past

Joe and Daisy arrived soon after lunch the next day. Joe had to carry Sally for the last part of the journey as she claimed to be too tired to walk.

'It certainly takes an age coming by bus,' he complained. 'I'd be quicker on the tractor, if we had any spare fuel.'

'We'll soon be back to normal, I expect,' Nellie assured him.

'Whatever normal was. I've almost forgotten,' Daisy said. 'We've brought you some eggs and a bit of butter. We couldn't manage anything else this time, I'm afraid.'

'That's very good of you. Thank you. It all helps. And your eggs are always so lovely. Really fresh and such big ones.'

Daisy handed over the shopping bag and Nellie took it to the kitchen. A whole dozen eggs! When you were only allowed one each per week, it was a positive feast. And fresh butter, again, much more than the usual week's supply. No wonder Joe and his family looked so well.

'Thank you again,' Nellie said as she returned the empty bag to her visitors.

'So where's our Lizzie?' Joe asked. 'Thought she was supposed to be here.'

'She's just coming. You'd better hear it from me. She's finished with Charlie. Broken off her engagement.'

'Why the heck has she done that?' Joe was shocked.

'I don't know. She won't say much.'

'Well, blow me down. There's a turn up.'

'Maybe she's met someone else?' Daisy suggested.

'She says not, but she did look a bit pink when we asked her.'

Sally started asking for something to play with. 'Why don't you go to the kitchen and see if Tom wants to play? You can go into the garden if you like, but don't go in the mud.' The little girl trotted off. 'She's growing so big, isn't

41

she? Lovely little girl.'

Lizzie came into the room looking calm and less stressed than earlier.

'Sorry to hear about you and Charlie,' Daisy said immediately. 'I was hoping we'd soon have wedding bells. Sally was hoping to be a bridesmaid.'

'Sorry to disappoint, but that's that. Now, tell me about life on the farm? How are your parents, Daisy?'

The conversation dragged on with some difficulty. Nellie had had enough.

'I'll go and see how tea's coming along. I'll have to help Jenny a bit. She's still single-handed, of course.'

By the time Nellie returned, Lizzie seemed to have recovered her good spirits and was regaling Joe and Daisy with stories of the awful matron who controlled the nurses with a rod of iron.

'I mean to say, what does it matter if a button is undone? Major crime to her and we get a severe telling off.'

'Depends which button is undone,' Joe said with a laugh.

'We're ready,' Nellie announced. 'I'll

just give James a call. He's working in his office, as usual.'

James found Nellie's family a bit of a strain, even after all these years. They might have come from a different planet as far as he was concerned. He knew nothing of farming and Joe's minimal education meant they had even less in common. Daisy was a sweet girl but had never been away from the farm except during her schooldays. He was at ease with Lizzie as she worked at the factory and he could appreciate her abilities as a secretary cum assistant. He came down when his wife called and fixed a welcoming smile on his face.

It was a pleasant enough meal and Nellie's egg-less cake soon disappeared. It may not have been the best cake ever, but in the circumstances, it had turned out reasonably well.

'I suppose you never have this sort of problem, do you, Daisy?' James asked.

'I suppose not. We are very lucky, but we do have to send all we can to the suppliers. We can't fall below the quotas or they ask questions. Just have to hope the cows give extra milk and the hens lay a few more eggs.'

* * *

'Well,' Lizzie said a little later, 'I shall have to get going. I'm on duty tonight and have to get my uniform sorted. No missing buttons or I'm up before matron for a final warning.'

'I'll come and see you off,' Nellie told her. The weekend seemed as good as over. 'It's been lovely to see you. Keep in touch and don't leave it so long next time. I'm sorry we can't give you a lift back.'

'No problem.' She swung down the road, her nurse's cape flapping.

'My little sister.' Nellie smiled fondly. 'I hope it's not too long before you come back to us properly.'

Joe, Daisy and Sally left shortly after Lizzie and Nellie waved them off and came back to help with the dishes. She was deep in thought, reflecting on how very much things had changed.

Her mother had lived with them for a couple of years after her dad had died. It had been a strange time. Her mother had never been quite at ease at Cobridge House and spent a lot of time in the kitchen with the housekeeper. It was totally unnatural to her to sit around all day after her busy life.

Once William had gone away to school, she was left with even less to occupy her mind. Ben going missing (presumed dead) had been the final straw and she had died soon after that.

As for Joe, he was the same lad who had escaped to live on the farm all those years ago. He could never face working in the mines or any of the options that were open to him where they lived. But, good for him, she thought. He had made his own life and done well for himself. He even stood to inherit the farm when the Bateses, Daisy's parents, finally went. Their lives were very different from her own and despite them all having exactly the same background, the Vale children were all completely different.

'You look miles away,' Jenny remarked as she came into the kitchen with a loaded tray. 'It all went well, didn't it?'

'Certainly did. Thank you for working so hard to make it happen.'

'Thank you for letting me be a part of it.'

'Of course you're part of it. You're family, aren't you? And I'm sorry if we sometimes forget that and put upon you too much.'

'Oh, Nellie, you must never think that. I'm so grateful to you for giving me and Tom a home and a living. I don't know what I'd have done without you. Well, I do. Same as most of the other poor girls left with babbies and no man.'

'There will be a lot of them, when things finally settle down.'

* * *

Lizzie got off the bus near the hospital. She glanced at her watch and hurried along. She would be late by the time she had changed into her uniform and have to face the wrath of matron. Mind you, she thought, with any luck she might sneak in while the shift was changing. Sister Cade was on duty this evening and was never quite so bad as the miserable matron. She rushed into the hostel and flung her cloak down. She changed into uniform, making sure all the buttons were fastened and ran across the yard to the ward entrance. So far so good.

She ducked into the sluice room quickly and began washing bed pans. It was a job everyone hated so she thought she'd earn some goody points for doing it without being asked. When she emerged, Sister Cade saw her.

'Where were you?' she demanded. 'I never saw you come in.'

'I was clearing up in there.' She nodded towards the sluice.

'Hmm, I see. Well make sure you

report to me when you come on duty. Otherwise I won't know if you were late or not.' There was a distinct twinkle in her eye. Rumbled, thought Lizzie, but she just smiled. 'I'd like to see you in my office before you take your break.'

'Certainly, Sister. Is there anything wrong?'

'Not at all. I'll see you in a while.'

Lizzie set to work doing the ward round. One of her friends, Joan, joined her and asked how the weekend had gone.

'Some good. Some bad.'

'Did you see your young man?'

'I did. That was the bad bit. I called it off with him. The engagement. He didn't take it well. But it had to be done.'

'Nurse. Stop chatting and get about your work. We have patients needing your attention.'

'Yes, Sister. Sorry, Sister.' They continued taking temperatures and settling pillows and continued their gossip while filling in the charts.

'And is that all because you fancy your chances with our favourite airman?'

'Course not. Things were over with Charlie months ago.'

'But you still like Daniel, don't you?'

'Not at all,' she denied, blushing near scarlet. 'He's nice and he needs a great deal of help. I'm sorry for him. It will be months before he's able to leave.'

'It won't, you know. He's being sent to Shelton Hall soon for rehab. I heard Sister discussing it with him.'

Lizzie went pale.

'Really?' she murmured. 'When's that going to be?'

'Quite soon. They've done all they can for him. Now he has to try and learn to walk again. That's what they'll do there for him.'

'I need to see him. Can you finish off in here?'

'Well, I can,' Joan replied, doubt in her voice. 'But you'll cop it if Sister Cade sees you.'

'I'm always in trouble anyway so I'm

not bothered. Thanks. You're a pal. See you in a bit.'

She scuttled along the corridor to the next ward and went straight to the bed of Daniel Miles. He watched as she came closer and broke into a wide smile.

'Now the day has just got a whole lot better. I missed you this weekend. Where were you?'

'I went home to see my family.'

'Just your family?'

'Who else would I be seeing?'

'Your young man, for instance.'

'I've told you before, there is no young man.'

This was the first time she had been able to say it without crossing her fingers behind her back. She'd been pretending for many weeks but now her conscience was clear. She had no young man waiting for her, anywhere. She had stopped wearing her engagement ring when she began nursing. It was usually hung on a chain round her neck, deep inside her uniform but nobody had seen it.

'I'm glad. If I wasn't a useless hunk of flesh, I'd even try flirting with you. Ask you out, but what would you do with someone as helpless as me? Lovely young girl like you.'

'You'll walk again. I'm sure of it. In fact, I heard you're going to rehab soon. Have you been told?'

'Yes. End of this week, I believe. I'll miss you, Lizzie.'

'And I'll miss you.'

'I suppose you wouldn't consider coming to see me one day? Or writing to me?'

'I might. I don't get much time off, though, and I'm not really sure if I would be allowed to visit.'

'You could always say you're my sister.' She laughed.

'I don't look anything like you. We'd never get away with it.'

'Then say you're my girl. Would you ever consider being my girl?'

'Nurse Vale. What do you think you are doing?' Sister Cade sounded furious

51

and her voice rang out across the ward.

Lizzie jumped.

'It's my fault, Sister,' Daniel said, his voice suddenly weak and persuasive. 'I called her over. I think I can feel some sort of movement in my legs.'

'That's good. But a junior nurse like Nurse Vale here is hardly one who can help or advise you. You'll see the doctor in the morning. Now, get back to your duties, nurse.'

Daniel raised his hand in a farewell gesture behind Sister's back and Lizzie left, stifling a smile. She almost skipped along the corridor.

He had asked if she would be his girl. She had spent the last few weeks flirting with him, well before he was sufficiently recovered even to realise it. She couldn't help thinking it was a little bit like when she and Charlie had first got together. If she went to visit him and Shelton Hall, she might be able to get to know him properly without matron or Sister bellowing at her. She still had to face Sister in her office in half an hour. What had she done, apart from spend time with the best-looking patient in the entire hospital? And Sister had asked to see her before that, so it must be something else.

'Nurse Vale. Lizzie, isn't it?'

'Yes, Sister.' She stood with her hands behind her back, twisting her fingers nervously.

'Matron asked me to have a word with you. I understand that you have your Higher School Certificate?'

'Well, yes. But that was a long time ago. Is it relevant?'

'Of course it is. It proves you have abilities. We're looking for girls with proven ability to move on to more advanced nursing qualifications. We've been recruiting anyone who could do the basics during the war years but now it's time for you to consider this as a full-time career. I know you've had your problems and often been in trouble for various misdemeanours, but I put that down to youthful high spirits. We'd like to put you forward for an initial interview. What do you say?'

'Well, thank you, first of all. But I don't want this to be my career. I hope I've done a good job but I really don't believe I have a vocation. I enjoy talking to the patients and helping out where I can, but nursing's not really for me. Besides, I have a job to go back to, once things are back to normal.'

'I doubt anything will ever be so-called normal again. But I suggest you give it some thought. You could have an extremely bright future in nursing.'

'Thank you, Sister. I will think about it but I'm sure I won't change my mind.'

'Very well. Oh, and Nurse Vale, please don't give more of your time to any one patient more than another. Is that clear?'

'Yes, Sister Cade. Very clear.'

She joined her friend, Joan, at the tea urn. Giggling over their tea, she recounted the interview she had just had.

'Me, doing this for ever. Have you ever heard anything so daft? Best of all, Daniel asked me if I'd be his girl.'

'Go on. What did you say?'

'I never replied. He wants me to visit him at Shelton Hall. Sister caught me by his bed and gave me a right telling off.'

'So what will you say?'

'I'll say yes; of course. Once he's left here, it will be quite all right. He won't be my patient any more, will he?'

By four o'clock in the morning, Lizzie was practically falling over with weariness. Normally when she had a night shift, she slept for part of the day, but being at Cobridge House, she had been enjoying the family get together instead. She was due to go off at six o'clock, but Matron arrived early and asked her to stay on for an extra hour. Past caring, she agreed.

'We have a new consignment of patients arriving. A small group of men recently released from one of the internment camps. They are in a bad way and some of them are suffering from mental problems. To be expected of course. I want some of my more experienced nurses available to help settle them.'

The military ambulance drew up at the main entrance. There were two porters and four nurses waiting. Matron had organised beds to made ready and they were taken straight to one of the smaller wards. When Lizzie had settled her own patient, she looked round to see if anyone else needed help. She stared at one man. A pair of blue eyes deeply set back in a very dirty, thin face stared back at her. Her jaw dropped as she went closer to him.

'Is it really you? How can it be?'

'Who are you?' he murmured before falling back on his pillow into unconsciousness. Lizzie sat down heavily at the end of his bed.

'Nurse Vale. What do you think you are doing?' snapped Matron.

'I may have seen a ghost,' she muttered. 'Or my lost brother has a double.'

'You Are My Brother'

Despite her exhaustion, Lizzie was unable to sleep. Was it really Ben, lying in a bed in her own hospital? Her first instinct had been to rush to the telephone and call Nellie, but she wasn't totally certain it was Ben and it would be foolish to raise any hopes.

Unable to rest, she went into work well before she was due the next evening. She crept into the ward where the latest arrivals had been settled and looked for the man who might be her brother. Round and round in her brain went the words from the fatal telegram. *Missing, believed dead.* How could they write that? If he was really alive all this time, why didn't they know? Surely all prisoners had their names listed and lists were sent to the War Office, or some such place?

'Nurse Vale? I don't think you are on

duty till the evening, especially not in this ward,' Matron sounded her usual angry sounding self.

'I'm sorry, but I needed to see one of the patients. You see, I think it may be my brother who was reported dead. Well, missing, presumed dead. It's amazing that he ended up here.'

Matron's expression softened.

'This contingent are from the North Staffordshire regiment. A small group of them were found hiding in remote mountains, we understand. They had escaped from a prison camp half-starved and some with serious injuries. They managed to survive somehow. Some have suffered mental damage and can barely speak. If your brother is among them, he has not yet been identified and I advise caution. Please do not tell your family until we are certain. Very well, Nurse, you may look and see if you do recognise the man. But remember what I said. Extreme caution.'

'Thank you, Matron. I think that one is Ben.'

She crossed to his bed and looked down at him. He was in a deep sleep but was breathing steadily. Thin to the point of emaciation, it was difficult to see her once-healthy active brother inside the form lying there. He must have been through hell. She glanced at his notes. There was no name attached and it seemed the main damage was loss of memory and starvation. Hopefully that could be rectified once he was home again. Nellie would be willing to give him a home and Jenny would be over the moon.

'Well?' Matron asked as Lizzie turned away.

'I really think it is him. I can't be one hundred percent certain until I hear him speak. I gather he doesn't have any papers or identification at all?'

'One of the men had a rather worn insignia on his tunic that was identified as the North Staffordshire Regiment so we assumed they were all from the same unit and they were sent here to be near their homes. Patience, child.

Patience.' She was unusually gentle in her approach. Maybe the tales told by the other nurses were wrong. Matron did have a heart beating beneath her starched exterior.

'Thank you, Matron. I may as well stay now and begin my duties early.'

'Very well. Report to the ward Sister where you usually work.'

Lizzie went through the rest of evening in some sort of daze. Several times she glanced nervously into the ward where the man she believed to be her brother was lying, still in a deep sleep. When Joan came on duty, she was surprised to find Lizzie already working.

'What's happened to you? Not like you to be so keen,' she said.

'That group who were brought in last night. I think one of them might be my brother, Ben.'

'But I thought he'd been killed?'

'The telegram said *Missing, believed killed*. They were found somewhere remote after escaping from some prison camp. It must have been before their names had been recorded. He's a very sick man, but mostly because he is starving. I think he should recover.'

'Oh, Lizzie. It will be wonderful for your family if he does. His wife will be so excited. Have you told them yet?'

'No. I'm not allowed, not until they have done a proper assessment and he can at least recognise me.'

'What a secret to have to keep.'

'It mightn't be too hard. I was there last weekend and so they won't expect to see me again for ages. Now, I must go and see if the gorgeous Daniel needs his brow mopping.'

'Just take care you don't get caught favouring any one patient,' Joan laughed.

Lizzie went into the next ward and watched as some of the men struggled to sit up. She went to help and pushed pillows behind them.

'Thanks, love, any time you want to, you can plump my pillows.'

'Behave yourself, Arnie!'

'Now then, boys, behave yourselves

or I'll have Sister telling me off again.'

She went to each of the beds in turn, leaving Daniel till last.

'I was beginning to think I'd offended you last night.'

'Of course not. Why would you think that?'

'Cos I asked you if you'd be my girl. Don't worry. I'm sure you've got dozens of men in your life. Gorgeous girl like you.'

'Daniel,' she said, feigning shock. 'Behave yourself.' He grinned and her heart flipped over. He was so good looking, and sitting up in bed, you simply weren't aware of his injuries. What was she doing even contemplating seeing him once he had left hospital? He might never walk again and if that happened he may never be able to father a child. Would that matter to her? She dragged her mind back to reality. She was jumping the gun somewhat.

'So, will you at least come to visit me at this Shelton Hall?'

'Course I will. I'd like to, really I would.'

'Does that mean you'll be my girl?'

'Let's not rush things. We'll see how you get on.'

'You mean see if I can ever walk again?'

'Let's just wait and see.'

'If you'll say yes, I will guarantee that I will walk again. I'll do everything I can to make it happen.'

'Good on you. Now, I must get on or I'll be sent packing and there'll be no chance of anything happening ever again.'

For the rest of the week, Lizzie was spending every moment she could between her two favourite wards. The senior staff members were surprisingly tolerant and allowed her to spend time with the man she now believed was truly her lost brother.

It broke her heart to see him with no memories except for the horrors he had experienced. He did not know who she was, except that she was a kindly nurse.

She tried to talk about their lives. About Jenny, his wife and Tom, his son. But he had never seen his son and might have been unaware that the child existed. A faint smile flickered in his eyes as she talked, but it was not a smile of recognition.

'Why are you calling me Ben?' he asked feebly.

'Because that is who I think you are.'

'But they called me Billy. My mates called me Billy.'

'Maybe they thought that was your name.'

'And who are you, again?'

'I'm Lizzie. Lizzie Vale. You are my brother.' Her voice was husky with emotion.

'That means you are my sister then? I didn't know I had a sister.'

'You have two sisters. There's me and then there's Nellie. Mind you, Nellie seems more like a mother than a sister, especially since our mum died.'

It was a long painstaking process, but he did look a little livelier each day and he was beginning to remember things that were said the previous day instead of Lizzie having to repeat everything over and over. The highest moment came when he said,

'Good morning, Lizzie. Are you still my sister?'

'Yes, my dear. I am your sister. And you are Ben Vale.'

'Ben Vale? I am Ben Vale.'

Lizzie felt tears burn her eyes but she blinked them back and gently squeezed his hand. She left the ward and went to the Sister's office.

'I think Ben is actually beginning to know me. I'd like to tell my family he's alive. May I have permission to do so?'

'I'll discuss it with Matron. When is your next day off?'

'Tomorrow.'

'Then if I can get an answer to you by the end of your shift tonight, you may be able to go home and tell them. It might be too much of a shock if you telephone them.'

'Thank you, Sister.'

She left the office and felt her knees go weak. The thought of going to Cobridge House and making this announcement was almost too much to contemplate. Damn, she thought suddenly. She had planned to go to Shelton Hall later the next day to see Daniel get settled in. But the news about Ben was much more important than her own, largely imaginary, romantic plans.

Permission granted, Lizzie caught the bus the next afternoon. She wanted Nellie to be at home when she broke the news and besides, she needed some rest after her exhausting night shift, so she had left her trip until four o'clock. Thank goodness she was back on days next week.

Though there was often less work to do at night, sleep patterns were totally compromised and she much preferred the day shifts when she could talk more to the patients. She walked along the quiet road to her sister's house, wondering how on earth she was going to break this news. She rang the

66

doorbell and then pushed it open and walked in.

'Lizzie? What a surprise,' Jenny said as she came from the kitchen. 'Why didn't you tell us you were coming?'

'I didn't know I was till the last minute. Is Nellie home?'

'Not yet. She won't be long. Do you want a brew?'

'I'll wait till she gets home, thanks. Everything all right? You coping with the war being over?'

'Hasn't made a deal of difference here. Still struggling to find summat to feed them on. Mr James expects proper meals to be served and there's nowt much to make them with.'

'I think you've done very well to manage anyway. Considering you were originally the nursemaid and had to learn everything in the kitchen from scratch.' She heard the front door open and ran into the hall.

'Lizzie? What are you doing here?'

'I wanted to see you.'

'I'm touched. So soon. Is there

something wrong?'

'No. Not all. Shall we have some tea? I want to talk to you and Jenny.'

'Jenny, too? What's going on?' She smiled sweetly and said nothing until the tea tray arrived.

'Sit down, Jenny. I have something to tell you. It's a bit of a shock but it's good news. Very good news.'

The two women glanced at each other, puzzled by her words.

'Ben's been brought into our hospital. He's lost his memory and he's very thin but I know it's him.'

'I can't believe it,' Nellie managed to stammer. Jenny went white as a sheet and promptly fainted clean away. Her cup fell to the floor and she slid down after it. Lizzie leapt up and put her head forward. Gradually, the girl came round and stared.

'Sorry, I broke the cup.'

'Get up slowly,' Lizzie instructed. 'It's all right. Sit down again and take a deep breath.'

'How can it be? I mean the telegram

and everything?'

Lizzie recounted the story as she knew it and the two listened with a mixture of relief and horror.

'When can I see him?' Jenny asked, tears streaming down her face.

'Not for a while. He is still very confused. He only just knows my name and called me his sister for the first time yesterday, but that's only because I've been saying it to him for the last few days.'

'You mean you've known for a few days and didn't tell us?' Nellie almost shouted. 'How could you?'

'I wasn't allowed to. Because nobody really believed it was him. He had nothing on him to identify him and he thought his name was Billy because that's what the others called him.'

'We must get him home here as soon as possible. He must come here, of course, and we need to feed him up. We'll get Joe to let us have some extra supplies and we'll even contact someone on the black market if needs be. I'll come back with you right away and we'll arrange everything.' Nellie had the bit between her teeth and wanted to get it all settled.

'Hang on, our Nellie. You can't do that. He's not well enough to leave the hospital. When he does leave us, he has to go into rehab. They won't let him go anywhere until they are sure he will make a proper recovery.'

'But he won't do that until he has proper food and care from those who love him.'

'He is getting proper food. Food that is right for him. He could die if you try to fill him full of rich food too quickly. Give him a few more days and you can visit him in the hospital. Try to be patient and take things slowly.'

'Does he know about me?' Jenny asked with a feeble voice. She was still shaking. 'And Tom? Does he know he has a son?'

'No, love. Nothing like that, I'm afraid. He might start to remember things at some point but it may be that he has to start from scratch and learn everything from the beginning.'

When James came home, the story was told over again. New questions arose and Lizzie did her best to answer them. Nobody even noticed what they ate for dinner and Tom was beginning to think the grown ups had all become very peculiar. Once he was put to bed, the four of them sat talking and planning. James fully accepted that one of the rooms should be turned into some sort of nursing station for Ben. After all, his own mother had been nursed at home in her final days.

'We shall need to get someone in to help. I expect Jenny will want to take over the nursing duties so we should see if we can get a cook-cum-housekeeper of some sort. See to it, will you, Nellie? Put an advert in the paper or whatever it is you do.'

'I used to use an agency but I doubt if she is still in business. I'll put cards in the local shops. That way we might get someone who lives nearby.'

'Wouldn't it be better to have someone living in?'

'I suppose so. But aren't we going to be filling too many rooms? William will be home for his holidays in a few weeks.'

'Surely there will be enough space. We have all the old rooms the maids used. They could be done up a bit and make somewhere nice for a person who needs a home.'

'Assuming we can find someone to do the work.'

'I think there will be a large pool of people wanting work soon. In fact, I dare say I could send round some of our people at the factory to do some decorating. We haven't got a great deal happening at the moment so they might as well be employed here. We'll have a good look around and see what needs doing. Isn't there some sort of sitting-room near the kitchen? Where Mrs Wilkinson had her rooms?'

'Well, there is. I've been using it for

me and Tom of an evening,' Jenny reminded him.

'Of course you have. Well, take stock, Nellie. See what needs doing and get things moving. Excuse me now, I've got things to do.'

It was his usual habit once supper was over. What the things were, nobody knew, but he could often be quite a solitary man. Nellie put it down to him being an only child, unused to family noise. Strange, they had only one son, too, but at least he was used to having Nellie's family around the place.

Lizzie had been sitting quietly for a while, evidently deep in thought.

'I'm wondering whether I should give up nursing and come home to help look after Ben,' she said suddenly.

'Really? But I thought you enjoyed it. You said you didn't want to come back to the factory for whatever reason.'

'Sister has suggested I take exams and become a fully trained nurse, but I said no. Though I feel I've done my bit for the war effort, I couldn't cope with their rigid rules all the time.'

'And what happened to not wanting to leave when I asked you at the weekend?' Nellie asked shrewdly. 'Could it be that some young man has left or is leaving the hospital?'

'Nellie, you are a witch. You always know what I'm thinking before I've even thought it myself.' Her sister smiled.

'And is he the reason you called off your engagement to Charlie?'

'No, not really. Nothing has happened except he asked me to be his girl. I hardly know him, but I feel there is something special there. But I'm not all that sure really.'

'What's wrong with him?'

'What, Daniel? Oh he can't walk.'

'Goodness me. You've given up your lovely Charlie for an injured man who can't even walk? Are his injuries permanent?'

'He's going to rehabilitation . . . well, he's already left today. I've promised to go and visit him.'

Nellie clearly thought she was out of her mind but wisely said no more. Jenny was sitting quietly all this time, wiping her eyes every few minutes as the news gradually sunk in and she was coming to terms with it. She had often dreamt of something like this but the dreams had always faded when she woke up. She spoke in a whisper the other two could only just hear.

'If he doesn't even know me, he might never want to see me again anyway. He might not love me. I mean, if he's injured, he won't even be able to work.'

'You're not to worry about that Jenny. You're part of this family and we have enough money to look after us all.' Nellie was reassuring. 'And anyway, once he's on his feet again, he may get his old skills back and then he can work at the factory, just as he always did.'

Lizzie yawned.

'I'm sorry, but I'm exhausted. I've been on nights all week and I haven't slept much at all since Ben came in. Is my bed still made up?'

'Of course. We left it after last weekend even though we hadn't expected you again so soon. Thank you for coming over. Much better than just getting a phone call.'

'That's what Matron said. Thought the shock might have been too much without someone to answer questions. Try to sleep both of you. Shame Mum wasn't here to share the news. Night.'

'Goodnight, dear. And thank you.'

They spent a busy morning looking round the house and making plans. Jenny had been sleeping in her old room next to the nursery and Tom used the nursery itself. There was another empty bedroom on the other side of these rooms and this was, they decided, a perfect room for Ben to use.

It needed decorating and freshening but would need very little work. Nellie felt quite strange when she went into the room she had shared with another maid all those years ago, when she worked in the house. But, if they were also decorated and refurnished, they would be quite adequate for someone to use. Efficient as ever, Nellie had a long detailed list ready to present to James when he came home.

Lizzie decided to leave soon after lunch and planned to visit Shelton Hall to see if Daniel had settled in. She also wanted to meet him in other surroundings to see how she might feel about him. Hospitals were such an artificial setting, where personal relationships were frowned upon and duty always came first.

For a girl like Lizzie, this was never a natural part of her make up. It had been said that she was too rebellious but she preferred the title feisty. It sounded good. Nellie had once said she could certainly have been a suffragette if she'd been around in those days.

Shelton Hall was once a large, almost stately home. It was built of the sandy brown blocks common in many grand houses of the area. Tall, well-proportioned windows ran all along one side of the building, suggesting large, high-ceilinged rooms would be found inside.

The owners of the Hall had passed it to the nation when their son and heir had lost his life in a flying accident. Elderly themselves, they had lost heart and moved right away from the area.

She walked up the long drive bordered by trees, many of which had been cut down, leaving fat stumps. Presumably the wood had been needed for something. Flower-beds were now set to growing cabbages, beans and peas and something she assumed were carrot tops were showing through. She approached the massive doors and looked for a bell. It was a long metal bell pull and when she yanked it down it sounded as loud as the sirens had once sounded at night.

She shrank back guiltily, wishing she hadn't touched it. Anyone trying to sleep would have been well and truly woken up.

A nurse in a stiffly starched apron

and rather large cap opened the door. Her manner was as stiff as the starch.

'Yes?'

'I've called to see Daniel Miles.'

'Do you have a visiting permit?'

'Well, no. I didn't know I needed one.'

'Well, you do. Visiting days are Thursdays and Sundays. Two till three-thirty.'

'But I'm working those days. I'm a nurse, too.'

The woman's disapproving glance at her clothing showed that she doubted the statement.

'And what are you to this patient? Are you a relative?'

'Well, no. Not yet,' she added, crossing her fingers behind her back to cancel the fib.

'I see. You are his lady friend then.'

'Yes,' Lizzie said, nodding vigorously.

'Wait there. I'll see if you can meet him in here. What name is it?'

'Daniel Miles. Air Force.'

'And you are?'

'Lizzie. Nurse Vale.'

'You can have ten minutes. As you are a nurse yourself and have duties during normal visiting hours, I'll make an exception. Don't let this happen again, though, and if you do come to visit, please use the side entrance and avoid ringing that blasted bell.'

Lizzie gasped at her words and then smiled.

'Thank you very much. I really appreciate your kindness.'

The woman sniffed and disappeared through one of the heavy oak doors set round the entrance hall.

'Well, well, well,' Daniel said. 'This is the sort of miracle I never expected. How simply wonderful to see you again. You led Sister to believe that we are betrothed!'

'I had to say that or she'd never have let me see you.'

'I'm flattered and delighted, of course. But you know nothing about me. How do you know I don't have a wife and seven children?'

'Because you'd have said something. Shown me photographs and talked non-stop about your amazing family. You haven't, have you? Got a wife?'

'No, Lizzie. How about you? Are you sure you haven't got a husband at home?'

'No. I was engaged once upon a time but that's all over now.'

'I'm sorry.'

'No need. It was my choice. We'd been engaged for years and never got anywhere. His parents were very demanding and I didn't think I'd ever cope sharing the same house with them.'

Daniel looked down. He touched his useless legs.

'I know it's early days for us, but you do realise I might never walk? I might be totally dependent on someone for ever?'

'I know. But you promised you were going to work very hard and do your best to make it happen.'

'Oh, you can bet your bottom dollar,

I shall. Especially with a girl like you to encourage me. I say, am I allowed a kiss? Now we're practically engaged?'

Lizzie leaned down to him and kissed him full on the lips. She had meant to kiss his cheek but he turned as she bent down and her aim was spoilt. Or, at least, that was what she tried to tell herself.

'Mm. That was nice. I might get hooked on you.'

'I certainly hope so. Look out, Sister is coming to take you away. I'm not sure when I'll be able to get over again. I'm on days for the next two weeks. But I'll write to you.'

'I'd like that. Goodbye and thank you for coming, darling,' he added for his audience's benefit.

Lizzie watched as he was wheeled away and smiled happily. For her, this was the best sign that the war was over. Her next call was to see Ben. Life was surely on the mend.

A Family Secret

Lizzie arrived back at the nurses' hostel at six o'clock. The evening meal was just being served and she couldn't wait to see Joan and tell her all the news. Her friend was astounded at her cheek in visiting Shelton Hall.

'I had to say we were practically engaged or they wouldn't let me in.'

'You've got a nerve, Lizzie. What ever did Daniel say?'

'He was fine about it and played it up beautifully. He even kissed me.'

'You really are a one. So it's all on, is it?'

'I guess so.'

'Finish with one man one week and start with another the next. I think you're taking a terrible risk. You hardly know him. You'd better watch it or you'll be getting a reputation.'

'Haven't I got one already? I've

decided that I'm going to give up nursing as soon as Ben is discharged.'

'I'll miss you. You're the one thing that keeps me cheerful. Have you been to see Ben, by the way?'

'No, not today. Have you seen him?'

'Briefly. There's no change. He just lies there staring into space. I did talk to him for a bit but didn't get much out of him. You don't think they'll take him to . . . well, the institution?'

'Over my dead body. No, we're getting organised at home and he can come back there. If I give up my job here, I can look after him. I can always do some work for my sister as well, and his wife is a nurse of sorts. We're getting it all arranged. Once he's got some of his strength back, he won't be stuck in bed. He'll be quite mobile again.'

'Best of luck is all I can say. Now, are we going to have some of this awful bread and butter pudding? I'm hungry enough to manage even that today.'

Gradually, over the next few days, Lizzie spent time with Ben and he began speaking more clearly. He was still very nervous of loud noises and shrank back into his pillows when any larger groups of people came into the room.

'I think we'll have you doing a bit of exercise today,' one of the doctors announced. 'Get him out of bed for a bit longer than he has been doing and have him walk along the corridors perhaps.'

'Certainly, Doctor,' Sister agreed. 'I shall let his own sister work with him. She seems to be getting through to him a bit.'

'Not usual for a family member to be involved, but I'll accept your advice. I'd like to get him moved on as soon as possible. The quicker we can get these men discharged, the better it will be.'

Lizzie was delighted when she heard the news. There was nothing wrong with his mobility, except for the fact he'd been lying in bed for so long without using any muscles. His legs looked very wasted and he lacked any strength.

Lizzie also persisted in asking if Jenny and Nellie could visit him. Finally, it was agreed that they might see him for a short time on the next visiting day. Delighted, she telephoned to give them the news. Someone had to be found to look after Tom as children were not allowed in the hospital wards.

An extremely nervous Jenny arrived at the hospital, dressed in her best clothes. Nellie was with her, a little nervous herself. Lizzie had primed Ben that they were coming and was also present for the visit.

She had given up her afternoon break so that she could introduce the women to her sick brother. He was sitting in the chair, wearing a shirt and trousers from the hospital laundry stores. The clothes hung off his slight form and she knew Nellie would disapprove and want him to have some new things.

'Ben, this is Jenny, your wife. She knows you may not recognise her and this is Nellie, your sister.'

'Hello, Jenny. Hello, Nellie.' His voice was expressionless.

'Oh, Ben. It's wonderful to see you again! I didn't think this would ever happen!' Jenny's voice was so full of emotion that they could scarcely hear her words.

Ben stared at her and tried to smile. It was heartbreaking to see that he clearly did not recognise her. She stifled her tears and smiled bravely. Nellie remained unusually quiet for her and stared hard at her younger brother as if she couldn't believe it was him.

Lizzie tried to encourage Ben to speak as much as he could. She prompted the others to tell him about things he might remember and ordinary, everyday things that filled their lives.

Occasionally, there was a slight flicker in his eyes, as if he was struck by a long-forgotten thought. Tom was not mentioned, as it was decided that it would be better to tell him about his son when he was more able to accept things.

After half an hour, he was clearly exhausted and Lizzie indicated to the others that it might be time to leave. Jenny had been holding his hand and was reluctant to let him go. She wanted to kiss him, but Lizzie caught her eye and shook her head slightly.

'Goodbye, my love. I'll come and see you again soon,' she whispered.

Nellie shook his hand and made some comment about being pleased to see him. She had found it almost more of a strain than Jenny had. Lizzie showed them out of the ward and stopped in the corridor outside to discuss the visit.

'He looked so old,' Nellie said tearfully. 'I could hardly recognise him. I don't know how you managed it when he came in, if he was looking even worse than that.'

'I knew him at once,' Jenny defended. 'I think he knew me, too, didn't he Lizzie?'

'It's early days,' she replied wisely. 'We have to give him time.'

'I'll send some clothes in. He shouldn't be wearing those awful rags.'

'Don't bother. The laundry washes everything and redistributes them every few days. Even if you did give him things of his own, they'd probably get lost in the general pile. You just have to be patient. I'm sure he'll soon be on the mend. I must get back to work now. I'll see you again soon.'

'Thanks, love. Nice to see you at work properly. You look very smart and quite unlike our Lizzie. Come and see us when you can. Or perhaps you'll be visiting your young man when you've got time off?'

'No such luck. I can only go there on two days of the week and I'm working then. I might try to get someone to change shifts with me soon so I can go.'

'So who's this young man?' Jenny asked curiously.

'Just one of my patients who's now left. Take no notice of Nellie's prattle.

She doesn't know anything. Must go. Bye, you two.' She kissed each of them on the cheek and went back to see how her brother had coped.

'Who were they?' he asked. She gave a little sigh and went through it all again.

It was another week before she was able to change her shifts and go to see Daniel. She had written to him several times, short, somewhat scrappy notes written late at night when she was almost asleep.

She had obtained the necessary visiting pass and on Thursday afternoon, arrived at the side entrance in good time for the scheduled hour. It was a glorious sunny afternoon and Daniel was waiting outside the doors, sitting in his wheelchair looking impossibly handsome. He was wearing his air force uniform tunic and had his hair neatly brushed. A light blanket covered his legs so on the surface, he looked as if there was nothing much wrong with him.

'Lizzie,' he greeted her with delight. 'Give me a kiss immediately. You look gorgeous.'

'It's good to see you, Daniel. You're looking really well. They must be doing something right in here.'

'Kiss, please. Now.' He pointed at his cheek and Lizzie glanced round to see if anyone was watching. She bent down to kiss his cheek and as before, he turned so that she kissed his lips. 'Nice,' he sighed. 'Shame I can't grab you in my arms and show you how kisses are meant to be. But, there's time for that to come, if you'll still see me.'

'So how's it going? Is the physiotherapy working?'

'I can move myself around really well now. My arms have grown stronger, so that's something. I can get myself in and out of the chair. Well, almost. The legs aren't doing much yet.'

'Do they hold out any hope? I mean, do they know why you can't move them?'

'They don't think my spine is damaged. But there's something not

91

connecting. I can't feel anything at all.'

She pushed him along the level path and found a shady spot beneath the trees where there was also a seat for her to sit down. She needed to be on his level so they could talk more easily. She learned a little more from him about the accident that had caused his problems.

He'd been trapped in his aircraft after making a bad landing. They had been worried he had sustained a crush injury that could have killed him when he was released, but he had survived. It was a slow business trying to make anything happen.

'Why is everything so slow when the body has to heal?' he asked.

'I don't know. It's the same for my brother. Everything is working for him except his mind. He can't remember anything of his past life and somehow, he feels he has no incentive to do anything much. Anyway, I want to know more about you. Who are you, Daniel Miles?'

'I have two brothers. I don't know quite what they are doing. I'm the youngest and so quite out of the loop for inheriting the family pile. But, as I am by far the best looking of my family, I'm sure to succeed somehow.'

His flippant words hid a deep feeling of panic, Lizzie thought.

'So what and where is this family pile?'

'My parents have a place out in the country. Daddy was in banking before the war. Not quite sure what he'll be doing now.'

His voice seemed to have changed to a different accent now they were alone. He had sounded more Staffordshire in the hospital. Now he sounded much more refined. Posher, Lizzie thought with a secret laugh. More like James, in fact.

'Do you mean to say you haven't been in touch with your family? Don't they know what happened to you?'

'Things didn't go too well when I last saw them. Blazing row over some sort of trivia. All very silly really. I left under something of a cloud. All in the past now. The future is all.'

'They don't even know if you're dead or alive? I can't believe it. They must surely want to know what happened to you?'

'Made it pretty clear that I was considered the black sheep of the family. *Persona non grata* and all that.'

'I can't believe it.'

'You said that before. I'm not worried. I can manage on my own or better still, with you to help me. Now, tell me about you and your lovely family. No rows and upsets there, I'm sure.'

'I'd rather get to know more about you. Tell me what it was you did to make them, well, kick you out of their lives.'

'I'd rather not. I want you to like me for what I am now and not be put off by my sordid past.'

'Now you really are giving me something to worry about. Did you walk off with the family silver? Or murder the butler or something?'

'None of the above. I'll possibly talk about it when we are on the verge of getting married.'

'If there's some deep dark secret you won't talk about, that day will never come.'

'Don't tell me that. I've quite set my heart on it. I'm merely waiting till I can walk you down the aisle on my own two legs.' Whatever his injuries, he had one of the most cheerful dispositions of anyone she had ever known.

'You really are leaping ahead a bit, aren't you?'

'Lizzie, Lizzie, you are the most gorgeous girl I've ever met. You are intelligent, caring and everything I could ever have dreamed of. I know you like me, or you wouldn't be here.'

'How do you know I'm not just sorry for you and want to help?'

'Because you're not like that. I can tell you like me for who I am.'

'But there's something sinister in

your background. Something you won't discuss.'

'It isn't anything so awful you'll never speak to me again, I promise. Now, can I say we will be engaged to be married some day soon?'

'Is that a proposal?'

'I suppose it is. But I simply can't do the down on one knee thing. Of course, if you insist, I'm sure there are some props around that could be used.'

'I'm not sure you are ever completely serious, Daniel.'

'OK. I get the message. You don't want to commit to a cripple. I understand that much and I must be completely round the twist to think you would. I hope you'll come and visit me again but as a friend rather than as my girl.'

'Oh Daniel, of course I will. I'm not saying I couldn't care for you. I think a lot of you and I think you're terribly brave to behave the way you do and cope with all you have suffered. Just accept that I am your good friend, for now at least. If there is something more ahead for us, then so be it.'

'Thank you for coming, Lizzie. Now I think I'd like to go back inside. Can you push me some of the way, please? We've come quite a long way into the grounds.'

Silently, they went back towards the Hall. Lizzie felt tearful for some reason. She had made a mess of it all, but engagement and marriage? That hadn't been on her agenda for many months or even years to come. She said goodbye and he had held out a hand to shake. No suggestion of a kiss this time.

'Would you like me to write to you again?'

'If you can spare the time.'

'And visit again?' she asked.

'If you can manage it. That would be very pleasant.'

Very pleasant, she reflected. Damned by faint praise. She caught the bus back to the hospital, thinking about the afternoon. It had been good in places but seemed to have gone awry towards the end. What on earth could he have done to cause the estrangement with his family? She could hardly believe anyone could break away so finally. And two brothers who didn't care?

It was all much too mysterious for her to leave alone. There was still some of the journalist in her and she knew she would never rest until she knew more about this man. On her next visit, she needed to discover exactly where in the countryside his home was. If it was in Staffordshire, she might be able to find an address in the telephone directory.

There was also the banker connection with Daniel's father. Perhaps James might have some contact who could answer some questions. If she could discover who his family were, she could write to them, as his nurse, trying to help him trace his family again ... or was it the other way round? She could find some reason to convince herself.

Over the next few days, there was

some progress with Ben. Jenny and Nellie made another visit and this time, emotions were less obvious. Her brother seemed to enjoy the company and another visit was arranged. There were also plans being made for him to go to the rehabilitation centre, when a place became available.

His physical strength was returning and he could now take walks unaided. It was good to see that he actually had the confidence to set off somewhere on his own. He was also spending time talking to the other men and, though the memory loss was still a problem, he was altogether more cheerful. Lizzie was delighted to see him playing cards with a few of the others one afternoon. That must mean some memory was returning, she realised. If he could play cards, he must remember some of the rules.

Though she had written twice to Daniel since her visit, she had heard nothing back. Nor had she managed to find anyone called Miles in the telephone directory. If only she had more time, she would like to go home and quiz James about how to track them down.

On impulse, she went to Shelton Hall unannounced, the following Thursday afternoon. She found Daniel undergoing his physiotherapy session in the large room used as a gymnasium.

'Yes, can I help you?' asked one of the staff.

'I came to see Daniel.'

'Oh, I see. He said that he wasn't expecting anyone his afternoon so we arranged his exercise session while we had a gap in the schedule.'

'I came on impulse. Unexpectedly, I managed to get time off from my own nursing duties.' She had quickly seen that a mention of being a nurse brought its advantages. 'I'm happy to watch for a bit, if it's allowed.'

Daniel had his back to her. He was pressing his arms against parallel bars and trying to make his legs move forwards. She watched the painful process and almost leapt forward as his arms gave way and he fell to the ground. The trainer helped him up again and brought the wheelchair behind him.

'That will do for today. Well done. Seems you have a visitor after all.'

Daniel swung round.

'Lizzie!' he cried out. 'Blast! You weren't here to witness that little escapade, were you?'

'It's all right. I've seen it all before.'

'But I'm trying to convince you that I'm practically on the verge of being able-bodied again.'

'I can see you're working hard at it. Now, shall we go and sit somewhere so we can talk?'

'All right. Isn't my girl a stunner?' he said to his therapist.

'Gorgeous, sir. You're a lucky man. I can see why you're inspired to work so hard.'

They left the gym and went along the corridor to a large sitting room overlooking what was a rather rain-sodden garden.

It was a beautiful room, with a number of comfortable chintz-covered armchairs. Daniel parked his chair alongside one.

'I didn't think you'd come again after last time. I'm sorry I was so rude. I'm sensitive to questions about my family and simply prefer to forget about them.'

'Very well. We'll concentrate on us and if there really is a future for us. For instance, what do you think you might do when you finally leave hospital?'

'You know, I simply have no idea. Obviously have to be some sort of desk job. I hadn't started on a career of any sort. I had been at university for just over a year when I left to join up.'

'Really. What were you studying?'

'Mathematics degree. I was expected to go into the family business. But being some sort of accountant never appealed. I wanted something more hands-on. An active occupation.'

'So, there was a family business, was there? I thought you said your father was in banking.'

'He was and may be still be. Look,

you're positively pushing me for information, aren't you? No wonder you had aspirations to be a journalist. I hope I don't find some article has been written about me and my private life.'

'Actually, I have been thinking along the lines of an article based on the return from war. More on how people can find a way to return to normal life.'

'Sounds as if it might be interesting, but won't there be dozens of such articles peppering the local rags?'

'You're probably right. But if I can just find an angle.'

'Thank you for writing to me by the way. I'm sorry I didn't reply. I felt awkward about it. I wasn't very kind last visit. I think I even asked you to marry me. Ridiculous idea. I hope you didn't take me seriously.'

'Of course not,' Lizzie lied. She went slightly pink. 'I knew you were just fooling around.'

'Jolly good show. We're all right then, are we? Good chums?'

'Of course. What else? But you can

still call me your girl for the benefit of the other chaps and the staff. It means I can get here to see you, too, without applying for another of these wretched permits. Honestly, anyone would think it was a jail sentence.'

'Must say, it feels like it sometimes. I'm imprisoned by my own stupid body.'

'My brother's improving by the day,' she said, trying to change the subject. 'He'll be leaving the hospital soon and going into his own rehab centre.'

'Might he come here?'

'No. His needs are different. Physically, he's OK, but he needs to try to sort out his mind. There are so many different sorts of injuries, aren't there?'

The rest of the afternoon passed swiftly and though Lizzie left in a happier frame of mind than the last occasion, she had to admit to feeling slightly disappointed that he said his proposal had been just a joke.

Was he simply trying to get out of it? Or was he afraid she had taken him too seriously? At least she now knew the Miles family had some sort of business in accountancy. James would surely be able to discover something about them. She must go home for another break as soon as she could.

As for getting engaged and married, they could think about that in the future. Hopefully, he was just playing a double bluff. If he thought she would leave the matter of his family break up, he really didn't know her at all.

Worrying About Daniel

During the following week, Ben was moved to a convalescent home a few miles away. It was very much a mixed blessing as it was more difficult to reach. It involved a short train journey and then a local bus and took up the majority of the day.

Nellie found one of the girls from the factory to look after Tom and sent Jenny to visit on her own. It was his wife, after all, who would eventually bear the brunt of his care and bringing him back to home. For Jenny it was all quite a drama and she felt very nervous of making the visit on her own. It was well into the evening before she returned. Nellie had cooked their supper herself and was keeping it hot until the girl came back.

'So, how was he?' she asked as soon as Jenny came in.

'All right. He did seem to know who I was this time but he still isn't my Ben yet. Goodness, I'm tired. That was quite a trek. I'd better get changed and get on with supper.'

'It's all right, Jenny. I've cooked something and Tom's already in bed. Go and say goodnight to him and then come down to eat with us.'

'Oh, that's wonderful. Thank you, Nellie. I'm ever so grateful that I don't have to start work right away.'

'Of course not. It's a very difficult time for you.'

Over the meal, Nellie and James learned of the beautiful place they'd set up as a convalescent home for the soldiers. As with Shelton Hall, it was another large country home that had been partially commandeered for their use. According to Jenny, it was several times the size of Cobridge House, which was generally considered to be one of the finest houses in their district.

'At least that means we won't be

taken over for military use.' James smiled.

'Mind you, if Ben comes here and even Lizzie's young man, we'll be doing a small bit towards being a nursing home ourselves.'

'So who's this young man of Lizzie's you're talking about?' he asked. 'I haven't heard about this one.'

'Some ex-patient who can't walk. She seems quite smitten but I doubt there's much future in it. She says he has nothing to do with her calling off the engagement to Charlie.'

'Oh, he was in today. Came to discuss the new letter headings. I felt it was time for a change now the war's over. He seemed all right. Said nothing about your sister of course.'

'Oh, I wish I'd known he was coming to the factory. I could have returned Lizzie's ring to him. I promised her I would do it and completely forgot.'

'That would set him off, I'd imagine,' Jenny remarked.

'I'll just have to face that when the

time comes,' Nellie replied. She heard the telephone ringing.

'I'll get it. Probably Lizzie calling to ask how the visit went.' She was correct about the caller.

'Nellie, can I come home again on Friday? It will only be one night as I'm going to visit Daniel again on Saturday afternoon.'

'Course you can, love. You know you don't have to ask. Any special reason?'

'Not really. Just want to see you all.'

'Jenny visited Ben today.'

'Oh, sorry I forgot. How did it go?'

'A difficult journey, I think, but she said he seemed quite cheerful and it's a lovely place.'

'Great. I'll hear all about it on Friday. Bye. Love you all.'

I wonder what she's up to this time, Nellie wondered. Lizzie always had an agenda.

Lizzie had confided in Joan, her friend at the hospital.

'There's clearly something terribly wrong, but I can't believe Daniel has a family who don't care what has happened to him. Can you imagine any mother not worrying about her son?'

'But he doesn't want you to know about it, whatever it is.'

'But how can I be serious about him if there is something wrong with the family?'

'Lizzie, I really think you should stop prying. You hardly know the man after all. Let it go. He's just another wounded casualty of that terrible war. For goodness' sake, you're taking it all much too seriously. Maybe he has got a wife or something hidden away. Maybe he just enjoys flirting with you and he doesn't want you to know his secret background.'

Lizzie thought about her friend's words. Joan was right to some extent. She didn't really know him, but even as she thought about him, her heart gave a little leap. This was different from the way she'd once felt about Charlie. She was just a kid in those days. Her first boyfriend, her first kiss.

She'd read somewhere that was always special and you never forgot it. She'd felt as if the world had stood still and she was floating somewhere above the ground. But, as the years had passed, those same kisses were without passion and she had never felt that wonderful feeling again for many years.

She dragged her thoughts back to the problem. What was this secret with his family? She just had to find out and the only way she could do this was by finding the family. She felt certain James would be able to help. She would do her research but would say nothing to Daniel until she had something positive.

She smiled happily. She was going to be the catalyst that brought the two halves of the family together. Surely they would be grateful one day?

'Do you know a company of accountants or bankers of some sort called Miles?' Lizzie asked James the moment she saw him.

'I don't think so, why?'

'I think Daniel's family are in that line.'

'You think? Has he told you they are?'

'Well, he hinted at it.'

'And why do you want to know this?' James asked suspiciously.

Lizzie thought carefully before she answered but decided the truth was best. Nellie was listening quietly, knowing she wasn't going to like what her sister was planning.

'He's had some disagreement with his family and says they don't even want to know how he is, even if he is still alive. I don't believe him and I think his mother must be quite desperate for news of her son.'

'I think you are entering dangerous territory,' Nellie told her. 'If he doesn't want contact with his family, then you should trust him.'

'I knew you'd say that. But all I want to do is to write to them and tell them the news. Please, James, please help me find them if you possibly can.'

'I'm making no promises. I could look in the trade directory and see if I can find anything. I agree with Nellie, though. You shouldn't poke your nose into other people's business.'

'Thank you, James. I knew you'd suggest something. If you don't want to be involved, I could come into the office with you and look for myself.'

'You're incorrigible, Lizzie.'

'I'm just a good journalist. Always seeking the truth.'

Nellie smiled. She gave a sudden jerk and left the room in a hurry.

'Nellie? What's wrong?' Lizzie called after her. 'Do you think she's all right?' she asked.

'I don't know,' James said helplessly. 'You're the nurse. You'd better go after her and ask.'

Lizzie ran up the stairs and into Nellie's bedroom. Her sister was sitting on the edge of the bed, looking waxy pale.

'Sorry. I must have eaten something that disagreed with me. I felt as if I was going to be sick. But I'm OK now, I wasn't sick.'

'You don't look OK. You look terrible. Should I call the doctor?'

'Course not. It was just something I ate, like I said.'

'I think you should lie down for a while. Shall I get you something? Water or maybe you'd like some brandy?'

'Certainly not brandy. A nice cup of tea would go down well. Sorry, it would happen just when you're home for an evening.'

'Good job it did. Looking at James's reaction, you'd be left lying in a heap if he was in charge.'

Being Saturday the next day, Nellie didn't have to go into work. James went off as usual, having reassured himself that his wife was in good hands. She protested that she was fine but finally agreed to stay in bed for her breakfast, though even one slice of toast was something of a struggle.

'And you wanted to go in with James this morning, didn't you, dear? To look in the directory.'

'It's not a problem. You're probably right. I shouldn't pursue it. Daniel will tell me when the time is right. Mind you, he said he would only tell me when we are about to get married.'

'Lizzie?' Nellie almost yelled. 'You're surely not thinking of marrying this man? You hardly know him.'

'So what if I am?' Her sister went pale. 'It's all right, love. I'm not. He did sort of ask me but then he said he'd only been joking.'

'Thank goodness. Please don't agree to anything rash. I know it may sound slightly glamorous to want to marry an injured airman, but you need to be very certain before you commit to anything. Think exactly what you might be taking on with someone who can't walk.'

'Oh, I know all about that. Everyone says the same thing. I do want to help him, I admit. But he's so lovely, Nellie. He is so good-looking and despite all the injuries, he's always cheerful and so funny. I'm certain he's a real gentleman behind the façade. I want to get to know him better.'

'There's nothing I can say that you'd ever listen to. But be careful, love. That's all I ask.'

★ ★ ★

Lunch, later that day, consisted of the inevitable soup and sandwiches. They all ate out in the garden as it was such a lovely day. Nellie seemed to have recovered and, somehow, there was an air of optimism about the place. James had searched through his directory and though he was uncertain that he was doing the right thing, gave Lizzie a piece of paper with an address.

Miles and Redfern, Accountants, Financial Planning and Advice. The address of the offices was Ashwell, near the Derbyshire border.

'Thank you so much, James. I promise not to do anything rash. I might be able to quiz Daniel a little more to make sure this is the right company. Not sure who the Redfern is, but it has to be connected to Daniel, doesn't it?'

'Possibly. But as we've both warned you, don't get involved with affairs you can't control. You may have the best motives in the world, but it's still meddling. And don't blame me if it all goes wrong.'

'The roses are looking nice,' Nellie remarked as if she wanted to change the subject. 'I was thinking we must try to get some flowers growing again. Make the garden a place we can enjoy instead of some sort of market garden.'

'Of course, dear. It may be a bit late for this year, though,' James said. 'I dare say someone would give us some cuttings if I ask around at work.'

'That's a good idea. Now, shouldn't you be getting yourself ready to leave, Lizzie? It's quarter-to-two and you'll miss your bus.'

The journey took almost an hour, giving Lizzie plenty of time to think. She was still determined to find some answers and to bring Daniel and his family back together. Her fertile imagination had been working overtime and she had every scenario passing though her mind.

The most worrying was that he had indeed got a wife or some sort of past problem with a woman. She even considered that he may have got some servant *into trouble* and shocked the family.

The bright day was clouding over as she arrived at Shelton House. The garden was crowded with the patients and their visitors and she looked around for Daniel. He must still be inside so she went to the side door and looked inside. Perhaps he was in the drawing room. He must have known she was coming and should have been waiting for her. She went to the reception desk and pinged the bell. A woman appeared.

'Good afternoon. I'm here to visit Daniel Miles. I can't seem to find him.'

'Ah, yes, he's in the ward. Not feeling

too well today, I'm afraid.'

'Oh, dear. Do you know what's wrong? Can I see him?'

'Oh, no. We don't allow visitors on the wards. There are too many really sick people there.'

'I am a nurse,' Lizzie told this dragon who was trying to keep them apart.

'Well, oh, I don't know. The rules, you know.'

'But I've taken time off and travelled quite a long way to see him. He'll want to see me, I'm sure.'

'I'll ask one of the Sisters if it's all right, you being a nurse and all.'

Half-an-hour later, she finally managed to enter the ward, under the strict escort of one of the nurses and found Daniel lying on his bed, looking very pale and drawn.

'Hello,' she whispered. 'Just what have you been doing with yourself?'

'Lizzie. How wonderful to see you. Help me to sit up, please.'

'Certainly not. You stay exactly where you are. I'll pull up a chair and sit near you. So, tell me what's happened?'

'I'm afraid I took a bit of a tumble. I was doing my best to get my legs working again and I simply fell flat on my face. Ridiculous, isn't it?'

'Where were you when all this happened? Not in the gymnasium, surely?'

'No. I was outside. Just thought I could make it to one of the seats. I planned to surprise you by sitting on an ordinary chair when you arrived. Stupid pride and this is what happens. I didn't think I'd be able to see you as I'm stuck in here.'

'I told them I was a nurse and you'd been my patient for many weeks. Seemed to work anyway. Have they assessed the damage you caused yourself?'

'Bruising in both body and pride. Don't worry. I've been severely scolded. I won't try it again. Golly, but you're a sight for sore eyes. Tell me what's been going on in your life.'

'Not much really. Work and more

work.' She told him about the previous evening and Nellie being unwell. 'She seemed fine today. But it's worrying. Nellie's never ill.'

'Maybe she ate something that disagreed with her. I'm doing it all the time in this place. Loads of things disagree with me, usually the staff. There's one of the physiotherapists who must surely have run one of those boot camp things. He's a terror. Here's me, doing my utmost best and he tells me I'm useless and just trying to waste his time. I ask you.'

'That's terrible. If anyone tries hard, it's you.'

'Thank you, darling. I knew I needed your encouragement to keep me going.' He tried to turn to be closer to her and reached out a hand. He winced with pain and lay back again, a fine film of perspiration covering his brow. Lizzie put her hand on his forehead. It was very hot.

'I'm worried about you, Daniel. You are in a lot of pain, aren't you? And you have a temperature.'

'That's your fault, darling. You're enough to send anyone's temperature through the roof.'

'Stop trying to make a joke of it. You need some medication and I think there's something you're not telling me. You have an infection of some sort. When did this accident of yours happen?'

'I'm not sure. Two, three days ago. It's not all bad, though. If I can feel pain down at my legs, it must mean there is at least feeling there.'

Lizzie said nothing. Many of the men she had nursed felt pain in limbs that had actually been removed. Phantom pains they were called. She kept her hand on his forehead and he touched it with his own hand.

'That feels so nice. I'm sorry to be such a wreck, love. I do appreciate you being here, really I do. Next time I promise I'll be sitting up in my chair, bright as a button and ready to walk you all the way round the garden.'

'I shall hold you to that, Daniel. Just you make sure you soon get better. I'd better go now. Back on the dreaded night shift again tonight. I daren't be late or I'll be up in front of Matron yet again.'

'Fate worse than death,' he murmured weakly as she gave him a peck on the cheek.

In truth, Lizzie wanted to see one of the doctors if possible, to find out what was actually wrong with Daniel. She was certain it was something more than a simple tumble. The duty doctor agreed to speak to her, though she had to fib a little and say they were engaged to be married.

'He seems so much worse than he has been lately. I really thought he was progressing so well, but now, he seems worse than when he was in the hospital.'

'I expect he told you that he fell down. He was foolishly attempting to move around without help.'

'I know that. He admitted it to me.

But he has a fever. He is clearly in pain and a lot of discomfort.'

'We're giving him what pain relief we can. As for the fever, it is the result of a minor infection. Again, we are treating it as best we can.'

'But I am very concerned about him. His morale is pretty low and I don't seem able to restore him to his usual good humour. He's always so positive.' She was near to tears and it showed.

'Look Miss, er ... I know it's distressing and the circumstances must be very difficult for you to cope with. Knowing someone who was always lively and full of fun and then discovering him injured, well it's something many people are having to cope with at these times. It isn't much consolation to you but at least he has come back. There are so many poor unfortunate men and women who did not make it.'

'Yes, I know. Thank you.' Clearly he assumed they had been together for much longer than they had even known each other. How long was it? Merely two or three months at most. Time had run together and she almost did not recognise weeks, let alone months.

'Now, if there's anything else?'

'Not really. May I telephone to ask how he is?'

'We don't encourage it. It takes up too much time for staff then to inquire about each patient and pass on results. Come again next visiting day and I'm sure you'll see a great improvement. We will always call you if there is anything you need to know. Leave a contact number with our reception desk.'

'Thank you, doctor. I appreciate your time.'

Lizzie walked down the long drive, her eyes still very moist. She felt very worried that there may be something seriously wrong with Daniel and that nobody was taking it very seriously. In a daze, she took the bus back to the hospital and went to change ready for duty. She just hoped she could stay awake long enough to complete her shift.

* ★ ★ ★ *

It was another week before Lizzie was free to visit Daniel again. She had done nothing about contacting his parents but was intent on doing so.

One piece of good news came from a call she made to her sister. It seemed that they were willing to allow Ben to make a visit home for a weekend. They would transport him by ambulance and collect him again two days later.

'So, if you can come home on Saturday,' Nellie had said, 'we shall be very pleased to get your help.'

She had to say that she couldn't make it and felt guilty that she was putting Daniel before her own brother. She convinced herself that Ben had several people available to fuss round him, while Daniel seemed to have nobody but her. She explained her dilemma to Joan.

'I could go and see Danny boy, if you like. Give you a full report.'

'They'd probably refuse to let you in. Thanks, though, love, it's very kind of you. No, I think the family will just have to manage without me. I think it's all getting so complicated these days, I'll have to give up nursing soon. At least I won't starve.'

'Lucky old you. I can't give up. I've got to work to earn money to help out the family. Not that I earn enough to keep a flea alive. Hope you can sort it out. And Lizzie, it just wouldn't be the same here without you. My life is so boring compared to yours.' They hugged each other before they set out for their last shift before the weekend.

To her great relief, Daniel was much improved when she arrived. He was up and sitting in his chair. They even managed a cheery conversation with a few laughs. Wisely, she said nothing more about finding his family, even though her curiosity remained unbounded.

'Do I get a kiss today?' he asked.

'Only I missed out last visit. I felt quite deprived.'

'You can have one when I'm leaving.'

'Two? To make up for last time.'

'We'll see,' Lizzie laughed, feeling like a mother with a pestering child. 'Have you been exercising this week?'

'Not much. I only started feeling back to my old self a couple of days ago. I'm all set to begin again on Monday. We get a day off from torture on Sundays.'

'You really do seem better, I'm glad to say.' She even told him about Ben's home visit. He was very pleased and surprised that she had chosen to visit him rather than go home to her brother.

'I had to come. I was so worried about you after last week.'

'Sorry. It was my own stupid fault. How's your sister, by the way? You said she wasn't well.'

'I haven't seen her. Nor did I think to ask how she was when she telephoned me. We were so taken up with Ben's visit. I hope it's going well.'

All too soon, the visitors' bell rang to indicate it was time to leave. Lizzie leaned down to Daniel's chair and kissed him, as properly as his position would allow. He sighed and reached for her again.

'Thank you so much for coming, Lizzie. I really enjoyed seeing you today and I can't wait for next week.'

'I'll come when I can. I may not be able to get away next weekend but I'll write to let you know.'

She waved as she walked down the drive. There were several other families leaving at the same time and she chatted to one or two other girls of a similar age. All of them had either brothers or friends in the same boat and they all complained about the restrictions on visits.

They wanted someone capable of asking the authorities for some changes and she nodded her agreement. She thought a petition might be a good idea, though personally, she would be very pushed to make it more often. Besides, she also knew some of the difficulties involved in maintaining a workable routine with visitors coming in and out.

Before starting her night shift, Lizzie telephoned Nellie to see how Ben's visit was going.

'He's all right. Clearly, he's pleased to be out of hospital but he seems very unsure of where he is.'

'Has he met Tom?'

'Of course, but he has no idea that he is the child's father. He seems to be enjoying playing with him, which is good, of course.'

'I'm glad. How's Jenny holding up?'

'She's very stressed of course. I think she's terribly upset that he still doesn't recognise her. James is finding it difficult, too, but then, he often does. How about you? Did you see Daniel?'

'Well, yes. I was very worried about him last week and I only had a little time to spare today. He does seem better again. I'm sorry I didn't come to see you all. Oh, and how are you? You were unwell last time I was with you.'

'I'm all right. Not really quite right yet. I think it may some bug I caught but nobody else is affected.'

'You should see the doctor if you're not completely better soon. We can't do with you being unwell.'

'I know. I will see him. I miss James's lovely Uncle Henry as our doctor. This new young one we've got doesn't seem to be quite as sympathetic.'

'You're showing your age if you think he's young. Doctors and policemen . . . that's the clue. When you think they look young . . . '

'Now then, Lizzie. I don't need you to tell me.'

'Must go. I'm on duty in five minutes and I haven't changed yet. Hope it goes well with Ben. Love to you all.'

Life Is Changing

Lizzie's next mission was to contact Daniel's family. He still said nothing about them or why there was a rift. She wrote a carefully worded letter to Mr and Mrs Miles, care of the business address she had been given by James.

Dear Mr and Mrs Miles,

I hope that I am writing to the parents of Daniel Miles. If this is not the correct family, then please accept my apologies and ignore this message.

I am a nurse at the General Hospital in Stoke and Daniel was recently a patient here. He was badly injured and is currently staying at Shelton Hall, where he is undergoing physiotherapy to aid his rehabilitation. If you require further information, you can contact me at the above address.

I hope this letter does not come as a shock to you, but I felt you should know his whereabouts.
Yours sincerely,
Lizzie Vale.

Hoping she had done the right thing, Lizzie stuck down the envelope and took it to the post office before she could change her mind. If Daniel was angry with her, so be it.

★ ★ ★

Nervously, she looked for the post each day, but there was nothing. Though she had written to Daniel, she did not mention the letter and nor did he reply. Perhaps he hadn't felt well enough, she told herself. In any case, she was not certain that the letter had found its correct target.

By persuading another nurse to swap duties with her, she managed to organise a visit to Daniel the following Saturday. It meant a very long duty the following day, but she didn't mind. She did feel slightly guilty that she had not visited her own brother and family.

When she arrived at Shelton Hall, she saw a rather tall, angular woman standing by Daniel's wheelchair in the drawing room. They were clearly arguing. As she approached, Daniel raised his voice.

'Here she comes now. Lizzie, meet my mother.'

'Mrs Miles. Pleased to meet you,' she said uncertainly.

'Lady Miles,' the woman said stiffly, declining the proffered hand.

'Lady?' Lizzie gasped. She looked at Daniel who was staring at her furiously.

'Indeed. Lady Miles. My esteemed mother, only she doesn't like to be called Mother any more. Not by me at least.'

'Lady Miles, I am very sorry if I did something out of place by writing to you. I had only the kindest intentions. I felt you would want to know about your son.'

'I should have been told earlier.' She sniffed. 'He chose to keep it from me, so I suppose I should show some slight gratitude to you for informing us. Everything I warned him could happen.' She paused and actually looked slightly upset. But the moment did not last and her haughty expression returned. 'I have offered to take him from here to somewhere more suitable, but he has refused the offer.'

'I'm sure they are doing all that can be done for him. They have an excellent reputation and they are getting good results from the many war-wounded who pass through here.'

'Your loyalty is commendable. However, you should not be meddling in affairs that don't concern you.'

'I'm sorry, but I do feel I am involved in your son's life.'

'Oh, dear me. Not you, too? I keep hearing about these young nurses pretending they care personally about their patients. I suppose you see it as an easy way out of this wretched profession.

Find someone rich enough and marry them. I expect you think you can somehow gain our gratitude for taking on such a burden.'

Lizzie felt her face going red and her fiery temper was needing a huge amount of control. How dare this woman be so rude? Lady or not, she had no right to disparage her this way.

'I would first point out that I have no intention of marrying your son. Somebody needed to show some care and respect for him. I understand there has been some sort of rift in the family, but . . .'

'Shut up, Lizzie. You have done enough damage already.' Daniel was almost bouncing in his chair with anger and exasperation. 'I asked you not to interfere but you just couldn't leave it alone, could you?'

'If there's nothing I can do for you, I shall leave now, Daniel. You can write if you need anything.'

Without any sign of affection, the woman turned and swept out of the room. Lizzie watched through the window as a large car pulled up outside the entrance and Lady Miles got in.

'Well, you're a dark horse, aren't you? Sir and Lady Miles as parents. What does that make you? Honourable or something?'

'How could you, Lizzie? How could you interfere like that? I specifically told you not to try to contact my family. You have no idea of the damage you might have caused. Now, please, just go. Leave me alone.'

'What? You mean you want me to leave? I've only just come. Well, almost only just.'

'I have nothing more to say to you. Not at present. I'll write to you if I can think of anything pleasant to say.'

Tearfully, Lizzie went off and walked up the drive, glancing back occasionally to see if he'd changed his mind and wanted her to return. But there was nothing. She had clearly blown it this time. How could she have got it so wrong?

She had been expecting to be the instigator of a happy family reunion with lots of kisses and hugs as she would expect in her own family. What could have happened to make this rift in the relationship between Daniel and his parents? Perhaps she would never know. Maybe she should have listened to Nellie and James's advice.

Lady Miles. The name ran through and through her mind. Surely that put Daniel right out of her reach? The family would never believe she cared and would always assume she was a gold digger, after his money. Mind you, she told herself, if he had broken from the family, presumably he had cast off any inheritance of any sort, as he intimated.

She gave a rueful smile. That was exactly what had happened to Nellie and James. His parents had believed Nellie was after the family fortune and had threatened to disinherit him. He'd been forced to return to the family business when there was nobody else to run it. Things had worked out for them in the end.

If she never saw Daniel again, how would she feel? The rush of tears to the back of her eyes told her. She would be devastated. Already, she knew that she felt more for him than she had ever felt for Charlie.

On her next day off, she went to Cobridge House to visit her family. During the week, she had become more and more despondent as each day came and went with no letter from Daniel. When she arrived, Nellie saw at once there was something wrong. She led her into the drawing room and sat her down on the large sofa and moved close to her little sister.

'Come on. Tell me what's wrong.'

'Oh, I've made a mess of everything, just like you said I would. I wrote to Daniel's parents and it all went so very wrong. Guess what? His mother's Lady Miles. Actually a Lady. She went to see him and it was like walking into an ice house when I turned up. She even had a chauffeur-driven car. They are really posh and I think their house must be something like Shelton Hall. You know, a really big place.'

'Goodness. But that shouldn't matter, should it?'

'I don't know. Anyway, she treated me like some trollop off the street and then stormed off, and Daniel wasn't much better. Told me I'd interfered in something I should have left alone. What on earth could he have done to alienate them all?'

'Goodness knows. It's probably something and nothing. Maybe he had a flirtation with one of the maids.'

'Oh, like you and James, you mean? Sorry.'

'Well, maybe.' She blushed slightly at the reminder.

'That's all a bit of an overreaction, though, isn't it? I mean, don't most of these youngest sons like to sow a few wild oats, as they say.'

'Maybe. How does that make you feel?'

Lizzie looked away.

'Enough of me. How are you? And Ben? Have you seen him again?'

'I'm not sleeping very well. Worrying about one hundred and one things. I'll be fine. Made of strong stuff, I am. I'm not sure how Ben's going to be when he comes home for good. They say it won't be long. There's nothing more they can do for him. As for work, it isn't picking up much yet. We're starting to make a push towards exports until things pick up here. We still can't use any decoration on the china, which I find unbelievable and very frustrating. Several of our girls want to come back to us but we can't take them on as there are no orders. But, there's talk of organising some sort of exhibition next year. Something to show the world what we can do.'

'So you're not in a hurry to take me back on?'

'Oh, I'd love to have you here again. Especially with Ben coming home. You could help look after him. We've also

141

got a new housekeeper starting soon. She's yet another war widow. Never really done much with her life but she needs a job and a home. She's called Wyn, a bit older than you. Claims she can cook plain food, but as that's pretty well all there is around these days, we won't complain. And William's home from school . . . my goodness, in just two days. We'll be quite a full house again.'

'Good. That will make things easier for Jenny. I'm thinking of giving up nursing anyway. I'd like to come back to work with you and then it should allow me more time to visit Daniel. That's if he ever wants to see me again. Some of the other visitors were asking if we could campaign to visit more often and a bit longer. Most time is taken in getting there and it's time to leave before you know it. I said I'd help organise a sort of petition. All a waste of time if I'm never going again.' She looked so miserable that Nellie put her arm round her.

'Come on love. If this was meant to be it will surely happen. I'll go and get some tea. Always helps even if it is the third time we've used the tea leaves.' It made Lizzie laugh.

'Reminds me of when we were kids. Remember how I used to have to make tea for Mum when she was ill? I must have only been very little cos it was way before I ever went to school.'

'You were only about four. We couldn't afford much tea in them days. Now it's rationing that stops us having a proper mash.'

'*They sounds reet Potteries when they taks like that,*' she laughed.

'Well, I'm glad you haven't completely forgotten your background.'

She sat looking out of the window while she waited for the tea. If she handed in her notice at the hospital, she could leave in a month or less. As long as she could earn something, she wouldn't need for much. She could carry on living here and James was always very generous in not charging her for board.

143

Mind you, her wages weren't that high at the hospital, considering the hours she was expected to work. She wouldn't mind helping in the house as well and would certainly be of use if she were there for Ben. Her mind was made up. She would really like her old life back, with or without Daniel.

She wrote the resignation letter the next morning and sealed it in an envelope ready to take to work. She thought she had to give a month's notice and so suggested the date to leave would be mid-August. Things were quietening a little as the stream of wounded soldiers was slowing down. Undoubtedly, the wards would be opening again to the public and operations on a wider scale would be resuming. She wouldn't like that so much so this was clearly the right time for her to leave.

Matron called her into the office during the next shift, after reading her letter.

'I find it hard to believe that you are actually resigning,' she said unsmilingly. 'You show promise, despite the many defects in your behaviour. Exactly why do you want to leave?'

'I always did have a job to return to. And my brother, Ben, is being discharged from hospital. He will need help for some time to come. I can manage my old job and his care quite easily.'

'I'd urge you to think again. This is an unwise decision and one you will not be able to reverse if it doesn't work out for you.'

'Thank you for your confidence in me, but my mind is made up.' Matron frowned and shook her head as if despairing.

'Very well. Then you may leave on August the fifteenth.'

'Thank you, Matron.'

'You can have two more days to reflect on your decision, in case you change your mind.'

'I won't.'

It seemed a long month with little to bring excitement. Ben was spending most of his time in his room. They were all looking forward to having Lizzie back at home to help draw him out of himself.

There was no news, no message from Daniel and several times she was on the verge of going to see him, uninvited. But her pride would not let her give way to her impulses.

At last August fifteenth arrived, coinciding with the day which became known as VJ day. The victory over Japan followed the hideous nuclear bomb and the devastation of Nagasaki and Hiroshima and the final surrender. Though relieved it was all finally over, there was still considerable shock about the way it was achieved.

It was a tearful farewell from Joan and some of her other friends and her usual patients called their goodbyes at the end of her final shift.

'I'm sorry it didn't work out with Daniel. You seemed quite smitten and I really thought it was going to turn into a happy ending,' Joan told her. 'Keep in touch, won't you?'

'Course I will,' Lizzie promised, knowing it was most unlikely. She left the nurses' hostel for the last time, carrying her small case.

'Well, that's it then,' she told Nellie when she arrived home. 'No more starched aprons and I can actually leave my hair loose. Goodness me, you're putting on weight, I do believe. It suits you. You're not pregnant, are you?'

Nellie grinned.

'I haven't had it officially confirmed, but yes, I'm fairly sure I am. After all these years, it's a bit of a miracle. You couldn't have come home at a better time.'

'Oh, Nellie, that's marvellous news. What does James say?'

'I haven't told him yet, nor William of course, so don't say anything. I'm waiting till I've seen the doctor next week.'

'Amazing, after all this time. You must be thrilled. At your age, too.'

'Hang on a minute. I'm not that old. Not quite thirty-nine yet. Just cos I've seemed like your mother all these years, doesn't mean I'm past it.'

'How far on are you?'

'I'm not sure. Probably about three months or so.'

'How lovely. It really is a new start for everything, isn't it?'

'I hope so. Have you ever heard any more from Daniel?'

'Not a thing. How to ruin a beautiful friendship in one easy lesson. Typical of me, isn't it?'

'Are you regretting breaking up with Charlie?'

'Not really. But it would be nice to have someone to go out with.'

'I'm sure he'd be pleased to see you. He still misses you, you know.'

'No. It wouldn't be fair. Do you think I should write to Daniel again?'

'Up to you. I'd leave it a while longer.'

'But suppose he's sent somewhere else? I'd never find him again.'

'Knowing you, you'll always find anyone or anything you set your mind to.'

'Thanks, Nellie. Now I'd better go and see this brother of mine.'

Ben seemed to have made himself quite comfortable in his little room. He had some books and a radio and was gradually getting used to walking around upstairs, if not often venturing downstairs.

He recognised her immediately, which pleased them both. He was also comfortable with Jenny, though not yet ready to assume his role as a husband.

It seemed that Ben had a real problem in accepting that Tom was his son. It was understandable as the two were never aware of each other's existence until now. But he was happy to play with the boy for short times. Nellie's son, William, now a very grown-up young man of fifteen, also found Ben difficult. Though they had always been great friends before the war, they had now grown far apart. The end of the war had not yet appeared to be the golden age they were all expecting.

After two weeks at home, Lizzie decided she would write to Daniel again. She spent a long time composing a brief letter, asking how he was progressing and suggesting he might like her to visit again. A couple of days later, she was rewarded with a reply.

Thank you for writing. I was pleased to hear from you. I didn't think you wanted to see me again, as you didn't reply to my last letter, he wrote. Lizzie stared at the words. What letter? she asked herself. *Of course I want to see you. You deserve an explanation for my dreadful behaviour. I know you interfered for what you thought were the right reasons but you should have listened to me.*

With love, Daniel.

She felt a warm glow. He wanted to see her and he signed it *with love*. It may be an easy way to end a letter but it was the first time he had put that. She ran upstairs to find Nellie and to tell her the good news.

'Where are you, Nellie?' she shouted. She tapped on her sister's bedroom door and went in. 'Oh, are you all right love? You don't look a bit well. In fact, you look proper poorly.'

'I'm feeling a bit rotten. Very rotten in fact. I'm afraid it might be the baby.'

'I'm fetching the doctor. Does James know about it yet?'

'Yes, I have told him. But nobody else. I'm not sure how William will take it so I've left it a while.' Her waxy pale face was moist and her usually immaculate hair lay in damp strings against the pillow.

'Just stay where you are. I'll call the doctor and then I'll bring you some tea, if you'd like it.'

'No, thanks, love. Just a glass of water. I couldn't face tea.'

'Now I am worried,' Lizzie said. 'You can't be well if you don't want a cuppa.' She stuffed the precious letter in her pocket and ran downstairs. She found the doctor's number written on the pad and called him. 'Please come as soon as you can. I am very worried about my sister. I think she may be losing the baby.'

She put the phone down and turned round. William was standing in the breakfast room doorway.

'What's the matter with Mum?' he asked crossly.

'She's not feeling well. I've called the doctor.'

'What was that about a baby?'

'We think she may be expecting a baby,' Lizzie said cautiously.

'That's disgusting. A baby at their age? And why didn't anyone tell me?'

'She was going to tell you when it was all certain. Nobody else knows. Well, your father does of course and then me. I'm the only other person and that's partly because I guessed.'

'Well I think it's terrible and I hope it does go all wrong.' His furious face told a story. He hated the thought that his role as the only son was being challenged. Typical boy of fifteen, she thought.

'You don't mean that, William. Please, give your parents the support they need at this time.'

'They should have told me. After all, I'm going to be the person most affected by this.'

'I really don't know why you should think that. I know it's been a long time but they always wanted to have more than one child.'

'Yes, but she's always looked after you and everyone else in the family. Why would she ever want another baby squalling about the place? We've already got Jenny and Tom living here and now Ben. And you've moved back as well. Why couldn't everything stay the same?' Red-faced and angry, he stamped off, slamming the front door behind him.

'Well, I handled that well,' Lizzie muttered. She hoped Nellie didn't find out what a mess it was, at least until she felt better. She collected a glass of water from the kitchen and told Wyn and Jenny that her sister was unwell and to expect the doctor soon. She went out before they could ask any questions.

'What was William shouting about?' Nellie asked when Lizzie went into the room.

'Nothing to worry you, love. The doctor will come as soon as he can. Here, take a sip of this. Are you feeling sick?'

'Sort of. I've just got cramps and I daren't move in case . . . well, you know what.'

'I don't really know anything about babies. I'm more used to dealing with injured soldiers.'

'And getting involved with them. You came bursting in before. Have you had some news?'

'Well, yes. I've got a letter from Daniel. He says he wrote to me, but I

154

never received it. He wants to see me again anyway.'

'That's great. I'm pleased for you. Now, about William.'

'I think that might be the doctor arriving,' Lizzie said and ran out of the room.

'Lizzie . . . ' Nellie called after her, but she ignored it. She went into the kitchen where there was an argument developing.

'Mrs Brownlow always made pastry first thing and left it in the cold pantry to rest. It's no good making it and rolling right away,' Jenny was saying.

'This is how I do it. And I am the cook here, aren't I?'

'Well, cook-housekeeper more like. I'm supposed to share the duties.'

'But aren't you supposed to be looking after the little boy and your husband, come to that?' Wyn was looking angry. They had all realised that she wasn't the best cook in the world but she was very willing.

'Now ladies, is there something

wrong?' Lizzie asked. Both of them began protesting at once and both, of course, knew they had right on their side. 'For goodness' sake. You sound like a pair of schoolchildren. Please, sort out your differences and consider Nellie. She doesn't want to hear things like this going on. Now, there's the doctor arriving.' The doorbell interrupted what might have been a long argument. The two women looked angrily at each other and Jenny stomped off up the back stairs to go and see Ben.

The doctor spent a long time with Nellie. Lizzie hovered outside the bedroom door, hoping she might be called in. At last, he came out, shutting the door behind him.

'I'm concerned she might be in danger of losing the baby. I offered to send her to hospital, but she refused, saying she had her own nurse right here in the house. You, I presume?'

'Well, yes, but I'm only a general nurse. I worked at the hospital till recently, nursing mostly the soldiers. I know nothing about pregnancy and babies.'

'Well, I'm sure you know the basics of hygiene, keeping her quiet and giving her nutritious food. She's entitled to extra rations during pregnancy, so please make sure she gets them. It's important that she rests for the next few days. She must stay in bed.'

'Right. I'll make sure she does. Thank you. But she will be all right, won't she? I mean, being that bit . . . older.'

'You'd better not let her hear you saying that. Her age should present no problems, but I understand she works at her husband's factory?'

'Yes, but I'm her assistant so I can make sure everything goes according to plan there.'

'Excellent. Well, I'll leave everything in your capable hands. Call me again if she has any further problems. I'll see myself out.'

'Thanks, doctor.'

She went back into Nellie's room and

shut the door. She repeated the doctor's instructions and suggested that the rest of the household should be told of her condition. 'I'll go into the factory this afternoon and check up on everything.'

'Thanks, Lizzie. You're a good girl. I think you're right. Jenny and Wyn need to be told, but I want to tell William myself. Can you send him up?'

'Actually, Nellie, he overheard me calling the doctor. He knows about the baby.'

'Blast. How did he take it?'

'Not well, I'm afraid.'

Plans Are Thwarted

Nellie turned out to be the world's worst patient. Everyone, except William, was delighted at the news and fussed over her, bringing her extra drinks and snacks until she was ready to scream.

Lizzie went into work at the Cobridge factory and tried her best to sort out the various problems that arose. The decorating shop, much depleted from the pre-war days, was in the good hands of the stalwart Vera, who had been in charge since the days before Nellie herself had worked there.

'Keep it to yourself, Vera, but Nellie's expecting. She's not feeling well and is confined to her bed. You can imagine how that's going down. Driving us all mad, she is.'

'Well blow me down with a feather. I am surprised. I know as how she always wanted another babby, but I'd have thought she'd left it a bit late for that. Oh goodness. I'm that shocked. Nice end to the war. How far gone is she?'

'Early days really So that's why I'd like you to keep it to yourself.'

'Course I will. So will you be doing her work? Not the designing of course, but all the rest?'

'Yes, of course. But I know I can rely on you to keep everything moving here. There won't be much designing to do in the near future, what with the Government restrictions. You can call me with any problems, or send stuff home with James when I'm not here. I might take a typewriter home to do the mail. I can stay there and make sure Nellie is behaving herself.'

'Give her my regards, won't you. And congratulations, of course.'

'Thanks, Vera. Good to know you're here.' Impulsively, she gave the older woman a hug.

'Oh, Lizzie. You're a good girl. It's lovely to see you coming in again.'

She collected a pile of letters and took it on herself to open them. Normally her sister did this and passed on those which needed replies. The bills for decorating supplies, she could pass on to the accounts department once they had been checked.

It was all quite simple and just needed a spot of extra organisation. It would save Nellie endless time and worries. Pleased with herself, she went home at the end of the day, before she had written her letter to Daniel. Visiting him would have to wait until Saturday now as it was Thursday tomorrow and she had things to do.

On Saturday it was a nervous Lizzie who finally set off to Shelton Hall. She had dressed in one of her smartest outfits, partly from Nellie's wardrobe and partly from her own pre-war collection. She wanted to look her best as she was hoping this was going to be make or break for her relationship with this intriguing man.

He was in one of the sitting rooms,

looking out hopefully in case she arrived. He saw the jaunty little hat first and his heart turned over. Her lively smile lit up the room as she came over to him.

'Oh, Lizzie! I can't tell you how pleased I am that you came. I was beginning to think I was never going to see you again.'

'It's lovely to see you, too. But I was surprised you said you'd written. I never received a letter from you, not until this week.'

'I sent it to the nurses' home.'

'I've left there. I'm now back at work at Cobridge. Well, partly at work and partly helping at Cobridge House.'

'I am shocked. I thought you were going to be a permanent nurse.'

'Certainly not. Too many rules and regulations. Besides which, I couldn't ever have got married. They don't allow you to be a married woman.'

His face fell.

'You mean you are thinking of getting married?'

'Lordy, no. Not at all. But I may want to one day.'

'That's a relief.' They smiled at each, neither knowing quite what to say next. After a few moments, they both spoke at once.

'You were going . . . ' Lizzie began.

'How are your fam . . . ' Daniel said. They both laughed again. Clearly the weeks since they last met had raised some barriers. Lizzie was burning for the promised explanation, but he was hesitant about bringing it up. At last she plucked up courage.

'Has your mother been to see you again?'

'Of course not. You saw how she was with me. I've decided it's now time to tell you the truth. Let's go out into the garden. I don't want anyone to overhear what I have to say. You look gorgeous, by the way. A real sight for sore eyes.'

He was wheeling his own chair, a pair of soft leather gloves on his hands to prevent him from becoming sore. He was skilled at manipulating the chair through doors and on to the ramp and only needed help when they moved from the path to the grass. They sat under a huge shady oak tree, the leaves dappling patches of sunlight over the pair.

'Are you going to tell me why there has been such a rift in your family? What could you have done to cause such damage?'

'Well, I told you I was doing a degree at university?' She nodded.

'Mathematics, didn't you say?'

'It was. I decided after a couple of years that I couldn't hack it. I told my parents I wanted to leave and they were instantly up in arms. Told me I was letting down the family and after they had spent so much money on my private education, it wasn't on. They couldn't force me to go back and made me go to work as a bookkeeper in my father's bank.

'That was even worse than being at college. At least there I could have some social life and, well, some fun. My brothers were all siding with the parents as they had got themselves well and truly involved in the business. The old man even managed to arrange things so they weren't called up to fight and tried to do the same for me. I found that unacceptable and decided to offer my services to the Royal Air Force. They threatened me with being cut off from the family if I actually went ahead. As you know, I did go. My mother said she never wanted to see me again as a broken wreck. Hence the comments that suggested 'told you so' when she came here.'

'Oh, Daniel, that's terrible. You were doing only your duty to the country.'

'Yes, well the son of that particular knight of the Empire should have been kept at home shoving columns of numbers around.'

'I'm so sorry. You can't think the sort of things I was imagining.'

'What? You thought I'd sold the family silver to settle my gambling debts?'

'That or something worse.'

'Oh, I get it. You thought maybe I'd got some maid into trouble?' Lizzie blushed scarlet and looked away. 'Heavens, you did think that? Oh, Lizzie Vale, I'm shocked. How could you have such a low opinion of me?'

'I couldn't think what else could cause such a massive break up.'

'You don't know my family. They'd probably think that was more normal. I hope this doesn't spoil things between us? I think such a lot of you. I know we joked about it once, but would you seriously consider being my girl? And by that, I actually mean would you consider being engaged to be married to an old wreck like me?'

'I'll think about it. Don't rush me, though.' Her heart sang with joy but she needed time. 'How are you actually getting on? I mean, are you improving at all?'

'I wheeled myself out here unaided, didn't I?'

'Yes, of course. Well done.'

'But that wasn't what you wanted to hear, was it? I can't stand, let alone walk. I can use crutches to move myself from one place to the next but that's more a sort of press up. They don't really think I shall walk again. I know that has many implications for the future. I also realise I am being very selfish in even asking you to share my life.'

'It is indeed a huge decision. I do care for you very much. I've been terribly unhappy these last few weeks when I wasn't seeing you and didn't hear from you.'

'But . . . I hear a definite *but* in your voice.'

'I do have a lot going on in my life at present. Well, I might as well tell you, even though it isn't common knowledge yet. My sister is pregnant and is in danger of losing the baby. I'm having to do a lot of work at the factory to stop her worrying and enable her to stay at home. And my brother, Ben, is still very difficult to cope with. Add to that my nephew, Nellie's son, has taken the news of this baby very badly. He thinks it's all quite terrible and selfish of them to ruin his life this way.'

'Ruin it how exactly?'

'Goodness knows. He's a fifteen-year-old boy, an only son. I think he feels his position is threatened in some strange way.'

'At least he's the male heir. Primogeniture won't be a problem whatever happens. I assume the parents to be are pleased.'

'Oh, yes, of course. But I don't think William has the least bit of interest in the pottery industry. Inheriting the factory would probably scare him to death.'

'So here's how I see it. I'm a poor war hero, sort of, disinherited by his family. No future. No prospects and my family think someone is only interested in him for his name and his fortune. You are part of presumably, a wealthy family with an heir who is also disinterested in his father's business.

Seems like we may have something slightly in common, somewhere.'

'If only you were passionate about the pottery industry. We could find you a job with James.'

'I know nothing at all about china. I have no talent of any sort. Maybe I could keep the books.'

'But I thought you hated that sort of thing?'

'I have to find something I can do if I'm to earn any sort of living. You know, I shouldn't even be thinking about having a normal life. I have nothing to offer anyone. Forget it. Just come and see me when and if you can. You can be my best buddy and go off and find yourself a nice husband somewhere the rest of the time.'

'Daniel, what are you saying? I thought we'd made up again? You're just too inconsistent for words.'

'I'm being realistic. You're a gorgeous girl. You're kind and caring but you're still young. You don't want to be tied to some old cripple stuck in a wheelchair.

Someone who might never be able to give you children or even have a normal married life.'

Lizzie stared at him. It was something she had been thinking about quite a bit, especially since she had known Nellie was pregnant again. Exactly how would she feel if she married someone who couldn't have children?

'I can see you are seriously considering my words. I really want to keep you as a friend but I don't think you should try to make it anything more than that.'

'All right. If that's what you really want. But I will give it some thought. I am very fond of you. In fact, I was pretty devastated at the thought of not seeing you again.' He looked away, his mind racing. He drew in a deep breath and tried to speak more normally.

'So tell me about your sister and this new baby.'

Desperately trying to keep things on a casual level, Lizzie chatted about all sorts of things. She talked about her past and the time she had tried to become a journalist. She told him about the articles she had written using a male pseudonym because she didn't think the editor of the paper would accept anything written by a woman.

'So, that was why you wanted to write something about the problems of returning home after the war? Just to keep your hand in.'

'Something like that.'

'I think you should do it. After all, you have plenty of experience. I don't even mind if you quote me. Coming to terms with injuries and everything. Coming down to earth with a bang. Literally,' he joked.

'I suppose when you joined up, you had a great time. Popular with the girls and all pals together.'

'There was a lot of camaraderie, granted, but also a lot of heartache. So many of us flew out and never came back. That's why we all lived life to the full when we could. All sorts of stupid pranks and risk taking. Good job we did really. Too many of my squadron never lived to tell the tale.' He looked so sad, Lizzie reached for his hand and held it tightly. 'That's nice,' he said with a smile. 'Leave it there. I like it.'

In the distance, the bell sounded for the end of visiting hours. Lizzie let go of his hand and started to get up.

'Stay a while longer. Pretend we didn't hear it. Unless you have to get back, of course.'

'It's OK. I'm not really in a hurry. I'll wait till someone comes and scolds us for hiding away.'

'Remember what I said, Lizzie. I really meant it. I'm no use to you even if I have fallen totally and completely in love with you.'

'What?' she almost shouted. 'What did you say?'

'Sorry.'

'You are a seething mass of contradictions. How am I supposed to cope with you telling me to find someone else one minute and declaring you're in love with me the next? I'm just totally confused now. I think I'd better leave before you say something else stupid.'

'I'm sorry, Lizzie. I shouldn't have said anything. Try to forget it.' She glared at him, desperately wanting to kiss him. Properly. Instead, she left him on the firm path after dropping a casual, almost sisterly peck on the top of his head.

She travelled back on the bus, deep in thought. If he did truly love her, how could she possibly ignore that? Round and round the options went. Love him or leave him?

When she arrived home, Lizzie found Nellie sitting in her chair in the drawing room. She was feeling much better and wanted to be part of the family again. She promised not to do anything but sit with her feet up and was anxious to know what Daniel had said to her sister.

'I can't go through it all now. Just accept that he did nothing wrong. I'll talk about it later when I've had time to think.'

She went to her room and took off

the little hat with its bright feather and tossed it to one side. She removed her jacket and kicked off her shoes and lay back on the bed. She was tormented by his words. One minute he loved her and the next told her to go away. She found tears rolling down her cheeks at the sadness of it all.

* * *

September arrived and before they knew it, it was time for William to go back to school. He had not enjoyed his summer break and was still angry about the baby. James remained as implacable as ever and took little notice of the frequent tantrums and complaints.

'I suppose this new brat will be here when I come back at Christmas,' he moaned.

'It won't be here until at least January,' Nellie told him. 'It will make next to no difference to you. You'll see. We shall have Jenny to look after it and I shall be at work as always. Everything will look better by Christmas. Just you wait and see.'

James had managed to scrounge some petrol and had decided to drive William to his school. He hoped that some time spent together might make the boy feel less aggressive towards his new sibling.

'I can remember how bad I felt each autumn term when I had to go back to school,' James remarked.

'It will be a blessing to get some decent conversation again. What with mother mooning around going all ga-ga about a new baby and Lizzie mooning around over her wounded airman, it's hardly been much of a decent break. Not even a proper holiday to ease the boredom.'

'I'm sorry, my boy. Nobody's been having much fun for the past few years.' His words did little to comfort his son and he felt sad to be parting on such poor terms. 'I'll try to get over at your next weekend off. We'll try to do something together. Just the two of us.'

'Thanks, Dad. Thanks for driving me back and for trying to help. Best of British. Must be worse for you than anyone, the whole place full of Mother's relations.'

'They're your relations, too. Don't be a snob about it.'

'I wish I'd known my grandparents. Your parents, I mean. I think I'd have liked them.'

'Maybe. They weren't the easiest of people, but it wasn't to be. They both died before you were born, so we shall never know. Right, well time for me to be getting back. You sure you can manage everything? Here's something to spend at the tuckshop, if there's anything to spend it on. You got your ration books safely?' He handed his son a note.

'How much longer will we need these ration book things? I thought the war was over.'

'It will be a while yet, I believe. Takes time for recovery. Goodbye now, my boy.'

'Bye, Dad.'

He looked quite forlorn, standing by the steps with his suitcase. James remembered exactly how it felt. He'd usually returned to school driven by the chauffeur-cum-gardener when he was young. His father was always too busy to spend any time with him at all, until he considered his son was needed to begin training for his role in the factory. Would William ever join them at Cobridge China? At the moment, James wasn't even sure if there would still be a company for his son to inherit when his time came.

The next few weeks formed a pattern for them all. Nellie went to work each morning and returned with instructions for Lizzie's afternoon at the factory. After the earlier scare, the pregnancy was moving along without problems, as long as Nellie rested in the afternoons.

Ben had improved almost beyond recognition, as the familiar routines came back to him. He had even visited the factory and was going to start working part-time very soon. As for Lizzie, she was visiting Daniel every Saturday afternoon. He had moments of depression, followed by periods of excitement when he felt some sort of movement in his legs.

Nellie went with her sister to watch a fashion show held in a local hall. It was organised as a fund-raising venture by one of the major stores. They were both excited by some of the new styles and especially by a new miracle fabric. They were all familiar with the wonderful innovative nylon stockings, but they were now making the fabric into blouses.

'Just imagine never having to iron again,' the commentator was saying.

'You never do your own ironing anyway,' Lizzie whispered. Nellie nudged her to keep quiet but gave a small smile.

The other items being promoted were a range of skirts. The ideas were interesting and quite exciting and best of all, some of the styles could be bought with only six coupons.

'They are gorgeous,' Lizzie whispered again. 'These peg tops look a bit like men's trousers with the pleats and buttons, but very smart, don't you think?'

'Not much use to me at present,' Nellie said with a sigh. 'I feel like a house end walking round.'

'And finally, we are promoting our range of evening skirts. What could be nicer than one of our graceful skirts and a pretty blouse. Nylon, of course,' laughed the compere. 'No more expensive evening gowns that you can only wear a couple of times. You can now vary your evening wear with our different blouses, saving money and those all important coupons. Thank you very much for your company. You can, of course, place your orders after the refreshments have been served.'

The audience applauded and a loud buzz of conversation followed.

'Just think, Nellie, you can buy a whole load of these things for when you start entertaining again. Different outfit every day.'

'And I suppose you'll decide exactly which colours I buy, depending on your own needs?'

'Well, it's always a good idea to be prepared, isn't it?'

'I have really enjoyed this evening. It must be the first time we've been out together for months.'

'Or even years,' Lizzie commented. 'You've been such a wonderful sister to me,' she said, clutching Nellie's hand. 'Thank you so much.'

'Oh, get on with you,' Nellie replied, touched by her comments. 'We're only too pleased to be able to help. But I've been thinking. You hardly ever do anything for yourself these days. You should get out sometimes. You used to love going to the pictures. Why don't you look up one of your old friends and go out? Go out dancing maybe?'

'All my old friends are married and have babies.'

'Then find yourself a nice young man to take you out.'

'Not many of them around any more,

are there? Anyway, there's Daniel. He may be able to take me out one of these days.'

'Oh, love. I hate to see you drifting through the years this way.'

'*Dunna fash thee sen*,' she laughed, using the old Potteries saying.

Once Ben was back at work, Jenny seemed to become restless. It was as if she no longer felt useful if she didn't spend so much of her day with her husband. The arguments between her and Wyn about how things should be done had continued, but they tended to keep them inside the kitchen so that the rest of the family were unaware of their problems. She dropped a bombshell one afternoon, when she went to see Nellie.

'Me and Ben, well we're very grateful for everything you've done for us, but well, we've seen a little house for rent and we've got a very good chance of getting it. We feel it's time we got on with our lives in our own place. We think we should qualify, Ben being injured and everything.'

'Oh, Jenny, you can't mean it?'

'Well, yes. I'm afraid I do. We only had our own place for a little while before the war started and you were kind enough to let me come back here when Ben left to join up. Then when we thought we'd lost him, it was good of you to let me stay on. But we have our own family now and we want our own home.'

'I can understand that, but I was so hoping you'd be here to look after the new baby when it arrives . . . In fact, I don't see how on earth I can manage without you. Jenny, please reconsider. We love having you and Ben here, especially now he's so much better. Almost back to normal, in fact.'

'That's just it. We want to sit by our own fireside of an evening. Cook our own meals. Well, I'd be doing the cooking, of course, but I'd decide what we were going to have.'

'I can see all that. Really I can, but I need you here.' Jenny looked as if she was about to burst into tears and Nellie tried to smile. She had been relying on the fact that Jenny would resume her former role of nursemaid and she would be able to get back to working full time again, just as she had when William was born. In those days, her own mother had also been around to help with the child. Now there was no-one else.

'I'm sorry, Nellie. You must think I'm very ungrateful. I hoped you would understand.'

'Do you think you'll be able to afford your own place? And food and everything else you'll need?'

'Ben's working and soon he'll be back full-time and earning a lot more, so we'll be fine. I could come and help you a bit but I wouldn't want a proper full time job again.'

'I see. When do you think you'd want to leave?'

'As soon as we've said yes to the house. It could be before Christmas.'

'But that's only a few weeks. Hardly any time at all. How will you furnish it?'

'We've got some stuff from before. It's stored in one of the garages.'

'Seems like you've got it all planned.'

'I know. Sorry. I'd better go back to the kitchen now. Make sure that Wyn is making the gravy properly.'

'You don't really get on with Wyn, do you?' Jenny looked away. 'Is it because of her you want to leave?'

'Only a little bit.'

'Suppose we were to give her her cards, would that make a difference?'

'Not really. I think we've decided.'

'If there's nothing I can say to make you change your mind, then you'd better get on with it. I'm not sure what I shall do. Maybe look for someone to come and live in, I suppose.'

'At least you'll have the nursery back and two more bedrooms left empty.' Jenny turned away and left Nellie, almost open-mouthed at the new problems she was about to face. A little terraced house instead of the comparative luxury of living at Cobridge House? Unbelievable.

At the factory, Lizzie was going along the corridor towards James's office, a sheaf of papers in her hand, she saw a man coming out of James's office. She stopped and waited till her heart regained its normal pattern.

'Charlie. What are you doing here?' she mumbled, shocked and confused to see him here.

'Just delivering some new designs to your brother-in-law. How are you, Lizzie? I've missed you.'

'I'm fine, thanks. And you?'

'Very well, thank you.'

'Good. And your parents?'

'They are living in a ground floor flat now. Very happy with it. I'm still trying to get round to redecorating and making my flat just that . . . my flat. It's somewhat empty at present as they took their furniture with them. But I have a chair and table and my own bedroom is as it always was. I manage.'

'Good. I know you must be pleased. It was what you were hoping for. I hope business is doing well?'

'Mustn't complain. I'm hoping everything will soon be back to normal. At least I was spared the fighting. I was considered to be in an important role as well as having my parents to look after. I did quite a lot of Home Guard duties, but then you knew that.'

'You were lucky. Well, I should get on.'

'I suppose you wouldn't like to go out one evening? A film or maybe just a drink?'

'I don't know. I'm not sure it would be a good idea.'

'No strings. Just for old times' sake.'

'I'll think about it. But I wouldn't want you to get the wrong idea.'

'Of course not. Just friends.'

'Thanks. I'll call you. Bye now.'

'Goodbye, Lizzie. It's great to see you again.'

She felt surprisingly affected by meeting him again. He was a lovely man, of that there was no doubt. But she knew she didn't love him. All the same it would be nice to go out somewhere with someone again. Nellie had been right. She should be going out more. Maybe a film would be harmless enough, as long as Charlie didn't set too much store by it.

Daniel's Determination

'I saw Charlie today, at work,' Lizzie told Nellie as soon as she got home. 'He's asked me out.'

'And will you go?'

'I don't know. I don't want to give him any false hopes but it would be nice to go out for an evening, just to make a change. Like you said, I'm not getting any younger.'

'Make sure he knows how you feel and it shouldn't matter. You might even fall in love with him again. You never know.'

'I won't. Oh, he's nice enough but I've grown out of him.'

'That doesn't sound nice.'

'What's up? You look pale. Is it that baby giving you problems again?'

'It's not that. Jenny and Ben want to leave. They plan to get a terraced house somewhere. I was counting on Jenny's help with the new baby. I suppose I'll have to get someone new and train her to our ways of doing things.'

'What a bind. Bit selfish of them, isn't it? After all you've done for them.'

'Maybe, but I suppose I can understand. I remember the joy it was to have this place as our own after James's mother died. Ben's certainly on the mend now and almost ready to start work full-time again. We have the go ahead to make vases and jugs again and some other fancy goods, so that will keep him busy once he's back up to speed on his potter's wheel.'

'Have a rest now. You look weary. I'm sure things will work out.'

Lizzie went up to her room and decided to turn out her wardrobe. Some of the things were totally out of date. She wished her mother was still here. She was good at sewing and could often re-work old clothes into something different. She would like something different to wear when she went to see Daniel on Saturday.

Maybe she should have a rummage through Nellie's wardrobe once more, though even that had been scoured for new ideas. He'd just have to put up with seeing the same old things again. Not that he would worry. He was only a man, after all.

When she did visit the following Saturday, she was given something of a shock. Not only was Daniel sitting in an ordinary armchair, but his wheelchair wasn't even nearby. A pair of cumbersome-looking wooden crutches lay on the ground beside him.

'Is this progress, Daniel Miles, or what?' she asked with a grin.

'It certainly is. But it comes with a sting in the tail. I am being sent out of here in a couple of weeks. They think I'm good enough to cope without their support.'

'Goodness. Where will you go?'

'That is in the lap of the gods. At the moment it seems my only option is to crawl back to the parents and see if they'll have me there. I totally dread the whole thing. I've been here for months now. It's like leaving one's boarding school and finding oneself cast adrift into the ocean of life.'

'But, but if you go there, I shall probably never see you again. Oh, Daniel, isn't there anywhere else you can go?'

'Not unless you have a nice level flat somewhere. I can't manage stairs, of course. Shame we haven't been married for years and already have a nice place of our own.'

'I wish. Wait a minute. My brother is about to leave our place. It's an upstairs room but maybe we could organise something downstairs. I'll give it some thought.'

'No, Lizzie. I couldn't possibly put myself on the mercy of your brother-in-law and sister. It sounds as if they've taken on too much already. And there's a new baby due soon. You are very generous, but I couldn't, wouldn't think of it. My own parents will have to take some responsibility for their own, personal black sheep. Besides, I'm expensive to feed and I can contribute nothing. Oh, I'll have a small war pension but that won't keep a fly alive.'

'When is it likely to be? Your dismissal from here?'

'Soon. No dates yet.'

'Please make sure you let me know. I don't want to come all the way out here only to find you've left. You have the telephone number, don't you? The Cobridge House number. Even if I'm at work, they'll take a message.'

'Of course. You gave it to me a while back. I simply don't know what the future will bring.' He clamped his mouth together in a straight line, clearly distressed but not wanting to show it. Lizzie knew him well enough to recognise the signs. 'So, tell me what you've been doing?'

There wasn't much to tell. It had been a case of spending the mornings at home, generally helping, doing some writing and then working at the factory in the afternoons. He made the comment that she should be going out having some fun.

'That's what Nellie keeps saying. I did meet Charlie at work this week. You know, my ex-fiancé. He asked me to go to the pictures with him.'

A look of slight pain flickered across Daniel's face but he smiled.

'That's nice. So, will you go?'

'I don't think so. He still cares for me and it wouldn't be fair because I don't share his feelings.'

'Oh, Lizzie. I hope it isn't just because of me. I know I have said things that should never have been said.'

'Don't flatter yourself,' she said as lightly as she could. 'It's my decision just as it was my decision to break off our engagement.'

'I know I joke about things like you being my girl and so on, but you shouldn't waste your life just seeing me once a week. That's soon going to change anyway. Once I'm back in the parents' stately pile, who knows when we'll meet again?'

'Don't say that, Daniel. I'm going to ask Nellie, anyway. You'd like her and James is probably your sort of person, too.'

'I'm sure I'd love them, especially if they're anything like you. But it really is time my parents took over my care. They've got enough money to run an entire hospital if they chose. Now, here's a plan. You could come and be my private nurse. That would be rather jolly, don't you think?'

'Oh, but I couldn't do that. I mean, well, I have to help Nellie and what with her baby due in January and . . . '

'Hey, it was only a silly sort of fantasy. A joke.'

'You might have meant it, though, seriously. I know you and your jokes. But I do have a job and once production at the factory gets going again properly, it's a full-time job.'

The afternoon was spent pleasantly enough, but Lizzie kept wondering if it was going to be the last they could spend together like this. When the time came to leave, Daniel managed to stand up, using his crutches and for the first time, she realised just how tall he was. Even leaning down to support himself, he was inches taller than her.

'Goodness,' she exclaimed, 'there's a lot of you. Somehow, I'd never taken on board your height. I should have realised when I saw your feet reaching the end of the bed.'

'I hope it isn't too much of a shock. I'd like to kiss you but I need to support myself.'

She reached up to him and kissed him full on the mouth. She hesitated, realising this was the first time she had been in control of the kiss. Previously it was always a snatched affair. She kissed him again. He grinned.

'That was a bit of all right. I'm glad I managed to stand for once. My legs are definitely getting some feeling back but it will be a long while before I can actually move them. Thank you, as always for coming to see me. I'll let you know if anything is going to happen.'

'I might try to get here on Thursday afternoon. I can try to make up the work during the evening or something. Bye now. And whatever you think, I am going to ask Nellie about you coming to Cobridge House. It's a nice place, if not quite a stately pile.'

He watched through the window as she walked down the long drive.

'Oh, Lizzie, Lizzie,' he murmured. 'I do love you so very much, but along with everything else I once dreamed of, I have to let you go.' He felt the dark gloom of depression sinking down on him again. He slumped back into his armchair, knowing that despite his huge effort to let Lizzie see him standing, he still depended on someone coming to fetch him with his wheelchair. He doubted he would ever really walk again and that took some accepting on his part. He knew that he needed to write to his parents and tell them of the situation. He had to have a place to stay and probably sooner than anyone had expected.

During the bus ride back home Lizzie's mind was working overtime. She mentally worked her way round the downstairs rooms at Cobridge House. There must be one that Nellie and James could spare. There was a cloakroom that Daniel could use. Perhaps some sort of bathroom could be added. She needed to find exactly the right way to broach the subject when she got back.

She was impatient to make something happen. When she arrived back, they were all in the drawing room having tea so there was no opportunity to speak to her sister at all. The atmosphere seemed friendly enough, with no sign of resentment from Nellie that her brother and sister-in-law were planning to move. In the short time between breaking the news and now, they had already agreed to rent their new home.

'I'm bored,' Tom announced after he

had been playing on the floor with some bricks. 'Can we do something now instead of talking?'

'I'll take him to the kitchen and find him something to do,' Jenny offered.

'I'll take him, if you like,' Ben said. Tom stared at him and stamped his little feet in a tantrum.

'No, no, no. I want my mummy. Not you. I don't know you.'

'He's your daddy, pet,' Jenny said softly.

'I don't know what a daddy is. I don't want him. I want Mummy. Just Mummy. Go away, Daddy.'

Jenny quickly took him away. Lizzie and Nellie stared in horror at their brother's stricken face. All the good things that had been happening over the weeks were suddenly lost.

'He has to learn that Jenny needs to share her time. It must be difficult for him to understand. You were a virtual stranger coming into the house and suddenly Tom is no longer the centre of Jenny's attention.'

'This blasted war. Does anyone ever get over it? The damage that has been done will never be repaired.' Ben got up and left the room.

'That was so ghastly to see,' Lizzie said with a sob. 'And I bet it's happening in many houses. Kids meeting their father for the first time and jealous because they are no longer the centre of attention.'

Lizzie sat quietly for a moment, considering whether it would be sensible to leave her request until the atmosphere had calmed down.

'How was Daniel?' Nellie asked after several moments of silence.

'Looking good. He actually managed to stand up today. I never realised quite how tall he is.'

'That's good news. So, do they think he will walk again soon?'

'I'm not really sure. He hopes so but it may just have been a brave show for me.'

'I suppose he'll be sent home soon, won't he?'

'Actually, Nellie, I wanted to talk to you about it. He has nowhere to go.'

'But you said his parents own some sort of large hall or something?'

'Yes, but his parents have disowned him.'

'Well, they'll just have to re-own him, won't they?' She watched her sister's face. She saw the turmoil going on and knowing her so well, immediately guessed what she wanted to say. 'Oh, no, Lizzie. No way. He simply cannot come here. What would people think? What would his parents think?'

'I don't know how you can say that. We've got oceans of room here.'

'Well, I'm sorry, but I don't think it can happen. James would never agree. It's not as if you're anything more than a good friend to the man.'

'But I think we might be much more. He keeps saying I should leave him but then he begs me go and see him again.'

'Well, there you are. You've done the classic thing. The nurse falls for one of her charges and he falls for his loving nurse. It's no basis for any sort of relationship except something casual.'

'Then I'll have to look for somewhere for us both to live.'

'Don't be ridiculous. How could you afford it for a start? Your pay at the factory isn't enough to live on. Only because you live here, rent and board free, do you have enough money to clothe yourself.'

'Then I'll have to get a job with better pay.'

'Grow up, Lizzie. Any well-paid jobs and such few there are, will be taken up by men returning from doing their duty for their country.'

'Like James and all those other friends of his?' she snapped, running from the room in a flood of tears. She'd show her sister. She'd go back to the newspaper and see if they'd give her a job.

Why shouldn't she and Daniel find a flat or something? She stopped suddenly. Was she assuming that this was what Daniel wanted? Perhaps secretly, he wanted to return to his parents' grand estate. She was such a fool. He had been trying to tell her in a polite and kindly way that he didn't want to live at Cobridge House in the first place.

Lizzie was almost silent during the evening dinner. Ben and Jenny had chosen to eat in the kitchen and so it was just James and Nellie eating with her in the formal dining room.

James noticed her frown and spoke directly to her. 'How is your life settling down again now things are getting back to normal?'

'I'm all right. I have a few problems that need solving but I'm sure I shall manage to get where I want to be in the end.' Nellie looked at her sharply but chose not to comment. 'If you'll excuse me now, I have things to do.' She folded her napkin and left the table.

In her room, Lizzie settled down to write a letter to Daniel. She had several attempts and finally threw them all away, thinking she might do better after sleeping on it. Somehow, she must get to Shelton Hall on Thursday afternoon, before anything happened that would make it impossible to sort out.

On Thursday morning, a letter arrived in the post. She recognised the writing and took it to her room to read in private.

My Dearest Little Lizzie,

It has finally happened. I am to be packed off from this illustrious establishment first thing on Friday morning. I have written to Sir G and Lady M to ask if they are willing to take back their long lost son. So far, I have not received a reply. If there is any way you can move heaven and earth to visit me on Thursday, we can bid each other our fond farewells.

Your ever loving, Daniel.

So this was really it. Her final visit to Shelton Hall. She went to tell Nellie that she was going into work for the morning and then going straight to see Daniel.

'That's good,' Nellie told her. 'I'm not feeling too well this morning. In fact, I think I might have to give up work for a while. I hope you weren't serious last week, about finding another job. I really need your help for the next few months. But I'm sorry about Daniel. You'll miss your visits there.'

Lizzie worked hard all morning, making sure the mail was up-to-date and she was even sorting out various problems usually left to Nellie's judgement. Amongst her mail was a hand-delivered letter from Charlie. He had left some work at the porter's lodge and left the letter to her at the same time. It was a simple request that she should give more thought to going to the pictures with him.

I want to see the new Gregory Peck film 'Spellbound', he wrote. I hear it's very good. It would be nice if you are free on Saturday, to go together. Ever yours, Charlie Swift.

Oh dear, she thought, I can't cope with this right now; and stuffed the page into her handbag. She would deal with it later. For now, she wanted only to catch the bus and get to Shelton Hall. She almost ran along the drive as if she was frightened that she would be too late. She rushed into the usual sitting-room but he was not there.

'Do you know where Daniel is?' she asked the woman who looked after the desk in the entrance hall.

'Oh, Miss Vale, isn't it? He is just about to leave us. His parents sent the car for him.'

'What?' she shouted. 'But he wasn't supposed to go till tomorrow.'

'That's correct. You may have noticed the car outside. It's rather grand.'

'The car?' she repeated stupidly. She turned and ran along the corridor and burst into Daniel's room. Two other patients were also in the room, watching the chauffeur packing Daniel's belongings into a large leather suitcase.

'Lizzie, you made it,' Daniel said with relief. 'Everything got moved forward and I didn't think you'd get here in time. The parents sent the car and Alfred here to collect me. They didn't tell me in advance so I couldn't let you know.'

'Well, it's a good job I came then, isn't it? So, you are going back to live with your parents,' she said pointlessly.

'Looks like it.'

'I hope it works out for you. I shall miss you terribly.'

'I shall miss you, too. I'll write.'

'I had made so many plans for us,' she suddenly burst out. The chauffeur stared at her and impassively continued packing things into the leather suitcase. Daniel saw her eyes turn towards the man.

'Even got the family crest on it,' he joked. 'The suitcase. Alfred brought it with him so my entrance back to the grand home shouldn't be marred by any of the scruffy, below par luggage I may have had.' He accompanied his words with a tiny shake of his head to indicate that he didn't want her to say anything in front of the servant.

'We shall all miss you, Danny Boy,' one of his room mates said. 'And we'll miss seeing your lovely visitor. You can always come and see us, love,' he added with a grin.

'I have to work, unfortunately. But I'll bear it in mind when I have a spare afternoon.' She smiled cheerfully at them, wishing she didn't feel as if she were dying inside.

'Thanks, Alfred. I think that's about it. You can take it to the car and I'll be out in a while. I have to collect some papers and things from the reception.'

'Very well, sir,' Alfred said.

'So what were all these plans?' Daniel asked her in a low voice so that the other men couldn't hear.

'Foolish nonsense, really. Just me living a little fantasy. You and I in some ground floor flat so you didn't have to manage stairs.'

'Oh, Lizzie. I am flattered. You know how I feel about you, but I'd be too much of a problem for you to have to look after. We couldn't afford to live decently and you would begin to resent me.'

'Never that. But I can understand that you'd hate living in some tiny flat. I was barmy to think it might even be possible.'

'You are just wonderful, Lizzie Vale. To think you'd even consider it means such a lot to me. I shall never know another girl like you.'

She felt herself sobbing and pulled out a handkerchief from her bag, trying to slow down the stream of tears that threatened. Charlie's letter came out with the handkerchief and fell on to the bed. Daniel picked it up.

'A letter from another admirer, no doubt,' he laughed as he handed it back to her. She blushed scarlet. Daniel stared. 'I'm right, aren't I? Is it from the Charlie you mentioned?' She nodded miserably. 'Good. Then at least I shall know you are not totally alone.'

'But I'm not planning to see him.'

'You should. Now, if you're willing to push me out to the front, I shall make my grand exit. Goodbye, chaps. My best to you all and hope you all soon manage to leave our luxury hotel.'

Alfred was standing by the door looking around what Lizzie had always considered a splendid entrance hall. His expression suggested it was inferior to the residence when he worked.

'Here are your papers, Mr Miles. And the remainder of your ration books. There is also a letter for your own doctor to tell him what medication you have been taking and advice on your future treatment.'

Lizzie insisted on pushing him down the ramp to the car, much to Alfred's annoyance. He wanted to take over immediately and see the young master to the car. He did, however, have to assist Daniel to get into the car. Lizzie leaned in to say a final goodbye. Daniel took her hand.

'Thank you so much for keeping me sane all these months. I'll never forget what you did for me. Darling Lizzie, you're a wonderful girl. Have a good life and be happy.'

Alfred stepped forward to close the door. Daniel waved and continued to wave and the car slowly drew away and sailed off down the drive.

An Invitation

Nellie was becoming more and more anxious about her sister. Lizzie had lost her sparkle and most unusually, was almost silent unless someone spoke to her. It was almost Christmas and it seemed there was nothing she could do to break her sister's silence. She began to feel guilty that she had dismissed the wild schemes to bring Daniel to live with them at Cobridge House.

The only signs of life came when the girl received a letter from Daniel. The crested envelopes were unmistakable and she ran up to her room with them immediately but would never comment beyond, 'he seems to be making some slight progress'. She then spent considerable time in her room composing her reply and took it to the post immediately it was finished.

'It isn't healthy,' Nellie remarked to

James one evening. 'And have you noticed how thin she's getting?'

'You're imagining it, dear.' All the same, he had noticed that Lizzie was looking very tired and drawn. 'I thought we should get her something special for Christmas.'

'Some jewellery, perhaps?'

'Certainly. I'll organise the jewellery shop in town to bring some pieces round for you to choose from. Perhaps when she's at work one day.'

Nellie had been busily organising the Christmas celebrations from her armchair. She had sent Lizzie on numerous shopping trips to find things particularly for the children.

Being stuck at home, she used her artistic talents to make a collection of beautiful decorations. The family already had a precious group of china baubles, specially designed and made in James's father's day. They were kept safely wrapped in tissue paper, a unique and almost priceless collection. To supplement these, she had made a number of hand-painted card and fabric pieces. A large box with all the things she was making was kept beside her chair and nobody was allowed a peek until Christmas Eve, when the tree would be delivered and they would all share in dressing it.

Lizzie was dreading the coming festivities. It had been almost a month since she had said goodbye to Daniel and it wasn't getting any easier. In his last letter, he had asked if she had seen Charlie again. He seemed to be encouraging her to see him again but she had no wish to do so. She preferred to stay in the house in the evenings rather than go out with anyone else.

Daniel's next letter arrived the day before Christmas Eve. He wrote about the plans for the festivities at their home.

Innumerable relations have been invited. There are several female cousins who were once high on the parents' lists as suitable prospects for

213

me. They probably won't look twice at me now, sitting in my wheelchair.

I hope you are seeing your Charlie over the break and that you are going to have some fun. I expect there will be parties at Cobridge House, too, so please make sure you enjoy yourself. Think of me sometimes, between your busy activities.

Happy Christmas,
Love from Daniel. xx

'Thanks a lot, Daniel,' she murmured. 'I shall certainly enjoy myself knowing you have a swarm of young ladies dancing attendance on you.' She went to the drawing room to join Nellie.

'Nice letter, dear?' Nellie inquired.

'Not really. He was full of the jolly time they were planning at his home. Loads of relations going there and parties galore, I expect.'

'We're going to have fun. Joe, Daisy and Sally are coming on Christmas Eve and are actually staying over till Boxing

Day. Daisy's father is doing the milking so they can have a proper break. And he's bringing a hamper of good things for us all to enjoy. Ben and Jenny are bringing Tom over for Christmas dinner so it should be fun.'

'I hope William cheers up a bit. He's been looking quite unhappy since he came home.'

'He wanted to spend Christmas with friends but James forbade it. He's agreed he can go over after the celebrations here. He's sulking in the hopes that his father will change his mind. Now, I want you to find one of my old dresses we can use to make some more decorations and if we cut into strips, I can use it to fasten round the presents.'

However much she tried to be involved with everything, Lizzie's mind was fixed on Daniel and his wretched female cousins. One of them at least was bound to fall for him as the rather glamorous, wounded hero. Presumably they were all wealthy and would employ servants to look after him. Torturing herself every few minutes did nothing to improve her attitude. When the huge tree was finally delivered on Christmas Eve, she set about helping to place it in the hall and became quite bossy as she took charge of it. Everyone except her was becoming excited and ready to make this the best Christmas ever. Once she had consumed several glasses of ginger wine, even Lizzie felt a little more cheerful. William managed a smile and sang along with the rest. His voice was almost broken but came out as a loud squeak occasionally, making them all laugh.

Sally hung her stocking up at the foot of the bed and was quite intrigued by the whole idea. She kept getting out to see if there was anything in it until she finally fell asleep. Nellie asked someone to place all the parcels under the tree and there was much excitement as people felt and tried shaking their gifts to guess what was inside.

Christmas day began early with Sally

shrieking with joy to find something had been delivered to her stocking. She ran into the room where her parents were sleeping, clutching the large sock. She was allowed to open it immediately of course and Lizzie went along to Joe and Daisy's room to share in the fun.

Everyone seemed delighted with their gifts and the air was filled with shrieks and thanks being called.

'This is for you, Lizzie,' Nellie said, as she handed over a flat box beautifully wrapped. 'Something special to thank you for everything you've been doing to help us through the years.'

Lizzie's fingers trembled slightly as she opened the black box to reveal a glorious emerald pendant.

'Oh,' she gasped. 'It's beautiful. Fabulous, in fact, but you can't give me something this expensive.'

'You deserve it, love. You've worked so hard for everyone at the hospital and here. Enjoy it and I hope you'll have plenty of occasions to wear it very soon.

You can start by putting it on right now.'

As Lizzie lay in bed late that night, still wearing her emerald, she reflected on the day. Much as she loved Daniel, she clearly needed to move on. He was way out of her reach.

A few days later, Wyn came in to say there was a telephone call for Lizzie.

'For me?' she asked. 'Who on earth can that be?' She went into the hall and picked up the receiver.

'Is that you, Lizzie? It's me, Daniel.'

'Daniel?'

'Remember me? I just wanted to hear your voice again. I haven't got long but I needed to know you are all right. You sounded very miserable in your last letter.'

'Now I've heard your voice, I am very much better, thank you. How about you? Are you progressing?'

'A little. Look, is there any way you can get over here? We're having a party for New Year's Eve? I'd love you to be here. You can stay overnight of course, but we can't manage the car to collect you. They have organised too many other demands on it for the afternoon.'

'Well, thank you. I'd love to come of course, but how will your mother take it?'

'I don't really care what my mother thinks. The girls that are staying are nearly all vacuous, unintelligent social-ites with no thoughts in their minds beyond clothes and fashions. I need someone who can really offer decent conversation. Now, about this party. If you have something special to wear, you'll knock their socks off. I know it's difficult with this wretched rationing. What do you say?'

'I don't know what to say. You're quite a long way from us, but I expect there are some trains.'

'Oh, Lizzie, does that mean you'll come? Say you will?'

'I don't know. Oh, all right then.'

'Lizzie, my darling, you'll be wel-comed with open arms. I'll call you again tomorrow, when you've found out about trains and things.'

'All right. And Daniel, thank you so much for telephoning. Just hearing your voice is so wonderful.'

She sat on the stairs for several minutes trying to come to terms with his words.

'Who was that, dear?' Nellie asked.

'It was Daniel. He's invited me to his home for a New Year's Eve party.'

'I see. And did his mother invite you?'

'I think so. He said she would welcome me anyway so I suppose she must know of the invitation. Oh heavens, whatever shall I wear? I hardly have anything remotely suitable.'

'But I'm sure you think I have?' Nellie smiled.

'I'm sure there's something. Can I go and look? It has to be something that will go with an emerald, of course.'

'You'll Win Everyone's Hearts'

It was late afternoon before Daniel telephoned. Lizzie had been to the railway station to ask about train times and which was the nearest station to Dalmere Hall. There were two trains that seemed suitable.

'I can be there either at three-twenty or five o'clock,' she told him. 'You are quite certain this is the right thing to do?'

'Of course I am. Make it the five o'clock train. I think there's someone else arriving about that time so you can get a ride with Alfred.'

'What, in that great big car? Won't he recognise me from the hospital?'

'Make it easier for him to find you. Don't worry, little one. You'll be fine. Just be your usual, charming self and you'll win everyone's hearts, see if you don't.'

'I hope I won't let you down. I'm not sure about my outfit. Just how posh is everyone going to be?'

'Oh, knowing them, they'll all try to outdo each other. You have youth and beauty on your side. If you came dressed in dusters, you'd shine above everyone else.'

'I'm going to wear something that is fairly new in fashion terms so I hope you'll like it. And Nellie and James gave me a fabulous emerald pendant for Christmas. I shall wear that of course.' She prattled on for a while and she could imagine Daniel's handsome face with that hint of a smile as he listened.

'Lizzie, I have to go now. The family are back from their outing. I can't wait to see you. Till Monday afternoon, then. Goodbye, my love.'

'Goodbye, Daniel.' She was still smiling when she went to the drawing-room to see Nellie. Her sister was dozing in front of the fire and woke with a start.

'Is everything all right?' she asked. 'I

don't seem to be able to stay awake for more than five minutes at a time.'

'Never mind, love, only about three more weeks and you'll be dashing around organising us all again.'

'Did Daniel telephone?'

'Yes. I'm to be collected from the station at five o'clock. Probably in that huge car Alfred drives.'

'How exciting for you.'

'Have you got a suitcase I can borrow? I can't travel in my evening clothes and I'll need something for the following day, anyway. Oh heavens. I haven't given any of that a thought yet. I'd better go and see if anything needs washing.'

'There are several suitcases in the box room. You can take your pick. I think William took one of them when he went off to stay with his friend this morning.' Her sister shook her head. What on earth would happen if she went away for more than a couple of nights?

'For goodness' sake, Lizzie. Calm

down. You'll be exhausted before you start the evening's events.'

'But you don't realise. These two days are probably the most important days of my life. If I don't make a good impression, I may never see Daniel again. If that happens, my life is over.'

'Don't be so dramatic. Now just sit quietly for a few minutes. Let's go through everything and you can check to see you have packed it.'

★ ★ ★

She left to catch the train at least half-an-hour before necessary. The weather had turned colder and snow threatened. She huddled into her warmest coat and wished she had an extra scarf.

The train was late arriving and would be even later arriving at Dalmere. Suppose they didn't wait for her? What would she do then? She could hardly walk there, lugging her suitcase along.

Outside Stoke, the train came to a

standstill. People were looking out of windows, trying to see what was holding them up. The story came back that there was were frozen points along the line. She could hardly believe her rotten luck.

It was another half-an-hour before they were moving again, by which time, Lizzie was a total bundle of nerves, twice as bad as she had been when she set out.

All was well. Alfred was standing beside the gate when she got off the train. She went to him and passed her case to him.

'Excuse me, Miss? I'm waiting for two of the Miles's cousins. I was not informed that you would be requiring a lift, too.'

'But Mr Daniel arranged it. He said you would be waiting for me as well as someone else.'

'Dear me. I'm not sure what I should do. I suppose you had better join my party then. I know you from somewhere, don't I?'

'We met at the nursing home when I was visiting Mr Daniel. The day he was leaving.'

'Oh, yes.' Did she detect a slight sneer? Too bad. All she wanted to do now was get into that warm car and be driven to see Daniel. The other two passengers arrived and they were finally on their way.

'I'm Elizabeth Vale, how do you do,' she said politely. *Elizabeth*, she thought? What am I trying to do? 'My friends call me Lizzie.'

'Hello,' the two women said without offering their names. They looked very superior and chatted to each other, quite excluding Lizzie from any conversation. How rude, she was thinking and hoped it wasn't indicative of how the next two days were going be.

It was quite dark by the time they drove up to the Hall. All Lizzie could tell was that it was a huge place. It was indeed similar to Shelton Hall in size, just as she suspected.

Nervously, she climbed out of the car

and followed the two cousins up the steps. She just hoped Daniel was somewhere close so that she wasn't left to explain who she was to some stranger, whoever that might be.

She glanced round to see if Alfred was carrying her suitcase inside. She had noticed the other two had left their own luggage in the car, so assumed that was the correct thing to do. Never had she felt so out of place.

It was a beautiful hallway, larger than the entire drawing room at Cobridge House. Oak panelled and with the staircase rising from both sides, the massive Christmas tree took up scarcely any of the space.

A woman in a black uniform greeted them and ticked names from a list. Lizzie's heart nearly stopped beating while the woman seemed to search for her name. Had she arrived unannounced? But she was there and was to be put in the small blue room, whatever that was. All the maids had taken the other guests to their rooms immediately.

'Lizzie, you're here at last,' came a shout from one of the doorways. 'Out of the way everyone,' Daniel yelled as he charged across the hall in his wheelchair. 'I was beginning to think you'd changed your mind.'

'The train was late and then it got stuck outside Stoke station.' She looked around, noticing everyone else had gone quiet. They were obviously wondering who she was to provoke such an enthusiastic greeting from the youngest son of the family.

'How are you managing, you poor dear,' one of the cousins asked him.

'Oh, hello, Julia. Frances. I hope you had a good journey here.'

'We were on the same train as . . . your little friend. So a positive nightmare of a journey. Fortunately, the heating in First Class is reasonable. The rest of the train must have been quite unbearable.' Julia looked at Lizzie, expecting confirmation, but none came.

'Come on, Lizzie, I'll show you round.'

'Thank you, Daniel.'

He led the way into one of the rooms. There was nobody else there and he beckoned her towards him.

'Come and give me a kiss. I can't tell you how much I've been looking forward to seeing you again.' He reached up to her and pulled her down to his face. He kissed her warmly and she felt her heart seeming to be exploding from her rib cage.

'Oh, Daniel, I've missed you so much. I was so afraid I'd never see you again and here I am, in your amazing home. It is quite magnificent.'

'You know something? I really hate it. I've had a terrible time since I got back here. They've fixed up some rooms on the ground floor just for me. I feel like I'm shut away in some sort of prison. Oh, it's luxurious enough, but I'm still some sort of pariah in this family. We must talk properly but it's rather late now. I'd hoped we'd have the chance for a talk first but the party will be starting in less than an hour and a half.

The Mater is something of a stickler for timing. We must all assemble in the drawing room for cocktails by seven-thirty. Dinner is at eight-thirty and then it's games and dancing for those who want to dance.'

'Goodness. It all sounds very organised. I don't even know which is my room yet.'

'I'll ring for one of the maids. Poor you. I haven't even let you take your coat off. Go and get into your finery and I'll be waiting for you in the hall. Somehow, I have to persuade this wreck of a body into my dinner jacket.'

'I hope I don't let you down. Seeing how grand everything is, I'm now extremely nervous.'

'You are the most gorgeous woman here, so even in sack cloth and ashes, you make a perfect picture.'

'You're very good for me, Daniel. I do love you, you know.'

'I know. I love you, too. Actually, I was going to save it for later but I'd like to announce our engagement this evening. What do you think?'

'Engagement?' she spluttered. 'You mean you're asking me to marry you?'

'Of course I am. Didn't you realise that was the whole idea of asking you to come here. We've both been so miserable while we've been apart. And when you said you hadn't seen anyone else since we parted, not even Charlie, I realised that perhaps I was wrong to turn down your offer to look after me. It's the only logical thing to do, isn't it? Now, what do you say?'

'It's all a bit of a shock. But yes, yes, please. I can think of nothing nicer than marrying you. But what will your parents say? And your family?'

'Congratulations, I hope. Actually, being the youngest son, they'll be delighted to have me off their hands. The only other problem is that I don't qualify to offer you any of the decent family jewels as an engagement ring. In fact, I'm not even sure if there is anything due to me. Sad, isn't it?'

'I don't care a hoot. If there's the odd

curtain ring going begging, that will do nicely. Oh, Daniel, thank you. I'm so happy and now I can face anything this evening brings, knowing I am your . . . your fiancée.'

'Darling Lizzie. Another kiss, please. Blast. I should be standing up reaching out for you, not stuck down here asking you to bend down.'

She grinned and bent down willingly.

'Thank you, my darling. Now go and change. We don't want to incur the wrath of the maternal parent at this point.' He rang a bell at the side of the room and a maid arrived moments later. 'Don't be long. Show Miss Lizzie Vale to her room, please. Do you know where you've been assigned?'

'The small blue room, apparently,' Lizzie replied. A glance was exchanged between the maid and Daniel.

'Not good enough. She can use the spare room in my suite. Make sure her luggage is brought down immediately. Come on, Lizzie. I'll show you the way.'

She followed him, still wondering

what was wrong with the small blue room. She asked and was told it was a room rarely used, at the back of the house and rather poorly furnished.

'I don't know what the housekeeper was thinking of putting you in there.'

'But a room next to yours, won't that raise eyebrows?'

'My darling, I intend to raise so many eyebrows this evening that they'll go right out of fashion. Now, open the door for me and we'll get on our way.'

Her room was plainly furnished, clearly designed for a male occupant. Daniel had explained that it was supposed to be used for some male companion his parents thought would be suitable for their invalid. Someone to take him out and entertain him so that the family were not burdened with the problem.

Lizzie was rather shocked by their attitude but remembering what she had been told, she could see they were trying to come to terms with a situation they hated. The maid arrived with her suitcase.

'I'm sorry, miss. It was unpacked in your other room. I've put everything back again and I hope it hasn't got creased. I can get someone to press things if necessary. Excuse me saying, but I really like your skirt. Very fashionable. Sorry. Please don't mention I said anything. I'll get fired if anyone knew I was making personal comments.'

'Thank you for the compliment. I won't say a thing. But it is nineteen-forty-five, you know. You're not some slave here.'

The maid smiled at her but the expression on her face suggested that she did not agree with Lizzie's words. She was a slave in a way.

'It's almost nineteen-forty-six, miss. Only a few hours to go.'

Lizzie took out her evening clothes and gave them a shake. The fabric had hardly creased at all. The silk blouse was slightly crumpled but the frills covered the worst of it. At least if the maid liked it, her outfit must compare with the other girls' things. Trembling with anticipation, she dressed quickly.

She brushed her hair till it shone and clipped it back with one of Nellie's best gold clasps. She hung the emerald pendant round her neck and stood back to look at the effect. She smoothed down her skirt, hoping the front slit didn't reveal too much leg. But, it was exactly what the best fashion magazine in Nellie's collection had said was *The Look of the Day*. Besides, she had the love of Daniel beside her. He was about to tell the world they were engaged. Well, if not exactly the world, his family and their friends.

She opened the door and peeped into the corridor. Should she go through on her own or was Daniel still in his room? Nervously, she went back into her own room and fiddled with her hair. She hung her clothes for the next day and her travelling outfit, shutting the wardrobe door as loudly as she could. Still making as much noise as she thought sensible, she left her room and went into the corridor, hoping he would emerge from his room. It certainly would not be done to knock at his door.

She walked slowly towards the hall and looked around. There was nobody there so she stood looking at the Christmas tree. There was a buzz of conversation from a room she supposed was the drawing room, but she was certainly too nervous to go in on her own. She turned tail and went back towards her room. She could say she needed a handkerchief or something.

'Where are you off to?' Daniel asked as he came out of his room.

'I was getting a . . .'

'You look sensational. I like the leg show. Wow. And you were looking for me because you didn't dare beard the lions in their den? Admit it.'

'You're right. I think everyone else is already in there.'

'Everyone except the parents. They

always make an entrance when everyone is assembled. The butler will be counting heads and waiting to tip them the wink. I bet we're the last.'

Heads turned as they entered. There was a moment's silence and the conversation began again. They were handed champagne and Lizzie took a glass for him, smiling as he wheeled himself to small group of younger people.

'May I introduce Lizzie Vale,' he said and rattled off a string of names she stood no chance of remembering.

The double doors opened and the hosts came into the room. There was a polite ripple of applause.

'Good evening to you all. Thank you for braving the elements to join us this evening. An auspicious occasion, I believe. A new start for all of us. Enjoy yourselves.' Another ripple of applause and conversations began again. Lizzie was quiet, overawed by the occasion.

She looked at the various fashions and for a moment, wavered in her own made-over outfit. Lady Miles had an amazing dress of scarlet velvet, worn with a necklace of a dozen or more large rubies. She was certainly a very striking woman, however much Lizzie despised her attitude to her son. At last, the buzz of conversation was interrupted by a dinner gong. She looked at her companion for a clue as to what they should do. He beckoned her to put her head close to his mouth.

'There is a strict order to go into dinner. The parents and guests of honour go first, then the two eldest sons and partners and then we go next. I suggest you push me as it will be easier. We're seated side by side instead of opposite each other, to make it easier than walking round the table. I assumed you wouldn't mind pushing me? I can manage myself, but with all these folks milling around . . . All a load of show-off nonsense, but one does as one is told in this house. Talk about pretensions of grandeur.'

She flashed him a quick grin and

followed the procession. Thank goodness he still had a sense of humour.

Though she was used to formal dining as it had once been at Cobridge House, this was an entirely different spectacle. One great comfort to her was the china. The table was set with a vast collection of one of Cobridge's most successful designs.

'My sister designed this service,' she whispered to Daniel.

'Really?' he said with surprise. 'That's amazing.'

'What's amazing, Daniel dear?' asked the cousin named Julia, sitting on the other side of him.

'Nothing. Just a comment I was making.'

'But it was something to do with the china,' she persisted.

'Lizzie's sister actually designed it. It's wonderful, eh?'

'Oh, amazing. Listen everyone, Lizzie here has a sister who is a potter. Astonishing, isn't it. We're sitting here with somebody who actually makes it.'

There was a pause before people began chatting again.

Lizzie was sitting with a face like fire. How could that woman embarrass her so?

'Thanks, Julia. Very sweet of you to draw attention to my fiancée.'

'Your what? Does anyone know about it?'

'My fiancée,' he said in a whisper. 'But it hasn't been announced yet, so don't spoil it for us.'

'Good god. You must be desperate.'

'Shut up, Julia. You're turning into a vicious gossip, do you know that?'

'And to think I once thought I might marry you. How the mighty have fallen. But then, you did fall, didn't you? From the sky by all accounts.'

'That's enough. Eat your meal and just keep quiet. Lizzie is worth a million of you.'

He turned away from her and concentrated on chatting to Lizzie. The gentleman on her other side had been chatting to her about the china with great interest. It seemed he was distantly related to the famous Wedgwood dynasty, though he had nothing to do with the china they made. Put at ease, Lizzie was able to enjoy the delicious food, even if she couldn't help wondering where they had obtained so much of what was scarce in everyone's lives.

'We have a large estate and so we produce our own food,' Daniel told her as if he could sense what she was thinking.

'Daniel,' she whispered. 'When are you planning to make this announcement of yours? Only I'm getting cold feet.'

'I won't allow that. Don't worry, Lizzie. I shall do it just when everyone is quiet for the countdown to midnight. Relax, darling. Enjoy your evening.'

'I'm not sure how anyone can dance after all that food. It was a wonderful meal, wasn't it?'

'I suppose so. After the extravagance of Christmas here, one gets used to it.

Now, shall we go the ballroom?'

'Ballroom? You mean you've got a proper ballroom?'

'I'm afraid so. The pretensions of Dalmere Hall go on and on. Do you shoot by the way?'

'Shoot? Certainly not. Why?'

'There's always a shoot here on New Year's Day. You could join in if you like. Take a brace or two of pheasants home for the family.'

'What, on the train? I don't think so.'

They sat close together in one of the alcoves surrounding the ballroom. It wasn't a huge room but a very beautiful one. There was a quartet playing at one side of the room, playing some of the music she recognised from the radio. Couples were dancing and when the group played one of the more lively numbers, more people got up and began dancing some of the American-style swing numbers, even some of them doing the jitterbug.

Lady Miles had seen the start of the dancing and rapidly retired from the room to the quieter drawing room.

'Shouldn't we speak to your mother before you make this announcement?'

'Probably not. Don't worry about it.'

'I think maybe it's all a bad idea. Let's keep it a secret for a while.'

'Are you having doubts?'

'No, not at all. I just feel a bit self-conscious among all these people who are obviously totally outclassing me.'

'Rubbish. Most of them are putting on airs and graces they have no right to. You're just as good as any of them and better than most. But if it really upsets you, I won't say anything.'

'I think that may be best.'

'Sebastian,' he said to a friend who was passing. 'Come and speak to me. Or were you hoping to ask my delightful companion to dance? I can't oblige and her foot's been tapping away all evening.'

'Delighted,' the handsome young man said. 'I'm afraid I don't even know your name.'

'I'm Lizzie. Nice to meet you.' He led

her on to the floor and tried to chat while the music was playing. She said yes and no a few times and hoped it was the right answer.

'Thank you so much. You dance well. I'd better return you to our friend there or he'll be challenging me to pistols at dawn.'

'Thank you. I enjoyed the dance.' She sat down again. 'You didn't need to do that, you know. I'm perfectly happy sitting with you.'

As midnight approached, Lizzie felt nervous. Would Daniel keep his word and leave the announcement for another time?

The matter was taken out of both their hands. Julia was quite unable to keep Daniel's comment to herself and had spread the word among a whole group of her friends. When everyone was grouped round waiting for the clock to chime, she called out,

'Go on then, Daniel. Tell everyone your news.' The crowd turned to look at him.

Making a huge effort, he rose to his feet, and unaided, told everyone that Lizzie had agreed to be his wife. Midnight chimed and there was a roar.

Happy New Year was mingled with congratulations. The cheers seemed to go on for ever. Auld Lang Syne was sung and everyone seemed to be kissing everyone else. Then a large, scarlet clad figure came to Lizzie and Daniel and a stony voice demanded,

'Into the breakfast room. Both of you. Now.'

There was a silence surrounding them and some slight giggles, especially from the women. Blushing a fiery red once more, Lizzie followed her hostess.

A Long Journey

'It was the most embarrassing moment of my entire life,' Lizzie said to Nellie after she recounted the details of that terrible interview.

Lady Miles had been furious that he chose that moment to make his announcement.

'It quite took away her moment of glory as the hostess. Apart from the fact that I'm so common . . . her words, of course . . . marriage was out of the question for someone who is no more than an invalid. Daniel bless him, stood or should I say sat his ground. He said I had shown him more love in a few months than he had ever had from his whole family in a lifetime. His brothers have, of course, married entirely suitable upper class girls with the right pedigree. Even produced heirs to the family pile immediately.'

'So where does all this leave you? Are you actually engaged or not?'

'Of course I am. Daniel was magnificent. Just because I left early, it means nothing. After the showdown with his mother, they miraculously found someone to drive me back this afternoon. Means I wasted my return ticket, but who cares?'

'So what happens next?'

'He's planning to speak to them properly once this party season is over. If they won't accommodate us then we'll have to find some other way to make things happen. We're very determined, you know.'

'I know you are, dear. And I wish you every happiness. Really I do. But I know something about marrying out of one's class. Once the dust settles, you have to learn a whole new way of life. Suddenly I wasn't the maid here, I was in charge of the whole house. James used to get angry because I didn't manage the servants as well as his mother had done. He conveniently forgot that I was also working full time at his factory.'

'Oh, did I tell you, they had the complete dinner service of your *Desiree* range? For about fifty people at least. I was very proud of you.'

'That might have made you feel slightly more at home.'

'I wouldn't go that far, but it proves they have some taste.'

'When are you seeing him again?'

'Haven't fixed anything yet. We'll see how it goes when he talks to the parents again. But he's going to telephone me each evening before dinner.'

'Well, I'm glad you're not too downhearted about it all. Do you think you'll marry soon?'

'As soon as it can be organised. I'm not going to let this engagement drift on for ever. I want to be with Daniel. We talked practically the whole night. He's always loved me it seems and was only trying to put me off so I wasn't saddled with an invalid. Not that he is an invalid. He just can't walk. But I'm sure it's only a matter of time. He stood last night. Completely unaided. I was so proud of him.'

During the next two weeks, Lizzie began to feel frustrated that nothing was happening. The fact that Daniel was totally reliant on other people to get about meant they had not seen each other again. His daily calls seemed cheerful enough and he remained optimistic that he would resolve things.

As the time approached for Nellie to give birth, Lizzie was kept very busy. They had persuaded Jenny to come in each day after she had the baby, but they had been unable to find another nursery nurse. Nellie would be looking after the new arrival herself for a while. With Christmas and New Year intervening, it had been difficult to organise interviews. They had, however, managed to find a new cook. Wyn was to take over duties as housekeeper rather than try to do both jobs less than successfully. They also had a cleaner coming in daily and hoped soon to find a new maid.

'Goodness, you'll be as good as Lady Miles any day now,' Lizzie told her sister. 'What's up? You're looking a bit green round the gills.'

'I think it's coming. Can you fetch someone? Anyone?'

'I'll phone for the doctor. And Jenny. Don't I have to get lots of kettles boiling at this stage?'

'Just get me to my room when you've made the calls.' She groaned and Lizzie decided at that very moment, that even if she could, she did not want to have a child, ever.

It was several hours later that Nellie gave birth to her second child. This time it was a girl.

'Isn't she perfect?' Nellie whispered. 'Our own dear little Beth.'

'Why Beth?'

'I wanted to name her after you, but we'd never cope with two Lizzies in one family.'

'Oh, Nellie. That's lovely. And yes, she is perfect. Simply perfect. Just like me, in fact,' she said lightly, hoping to cover the deep emotions she was feeling.

For the next few days it was non-stop for Lizzie. She was practically running the decorating shop at the factory and doing all she could to help Nellie at home. However busy she was, she made sure she was always near the telephone for Daniel's call.

'Do you think you could come over here on Saturday?' he asked one evening.

'Over to Dalmere Hall? You are joking.'

'No, I'm not. I really want you to be here. My parents are beginning to realise that I am quite serious in wanting to marry you and they know they, nor anyone else, are not going to change my mind. I want them to get to know you. My amazing, wonderful Lizzie.'

'I suppose I could. But it's rather a long journey with trains and buses to cope with on Saturday, too. Just when all the football crowds are starting to mill around.'

'I'll try to get someone to drive me over to collect you. Please say yes.'

'Well, all right.'

'And you'll stay the night, won't you?'

'Oh, I'm not sure about that.'

'You must or you'll be going home as soon as you arrive.'

She agreed to his request and spent the rest of the week regretting it. Nellie did her best to reassure her that it would be fine. After all, nobody could have been worse than the late Mrs Cobridge and Nellie had lived to tell the tale. Once more Lizzie packed her overnight bag and included a reasonably posh frock in case there was a formal dinner.

'I hate all this nonsense with particular clothes for this and that. At least the war has meant we don't have to spend half our lives changing outfits. Right, well I think that's everything I can possibly need. Oh, do you think I should take another hat in case we go to church tomorrow?'

'If you're travelling by car you can easily take one, can't you? Now go and get yourself near the door ready for his arrival.'

'Do you want to meet him? I mean, should I invite him in?'

'If you'd like to. But I suspect he'll want to get you back to his place. It looks as if it will be a rather important meeting. Hold your head high girl. Be proud. You're a lovely young woman from excellent stock.'

'Thanks, Nellie. I do love you.'

'Get on with you. Have a lovely time and don't let them get to you. You're as good, if not better, than any of them.'

It was a friend who drove Daniel in a relatively modest little saloon car. Lizzie saw it stop outside and immediately went out to meet them.

'Darling. You look wonderful,' Daniel called through his window.

'Hello, both of you. Do you want to come inside or are you in a hurry?'

'I'd like us to get back. Mamma is providing luncheon and we'll get off to a bad start if we're late. This is Freddy, by the way. A good chum of mine who's had his arm twisted to drive me around.'

The drive to Dalmere took under an hour, considerably less than the two-hour train journey she had made last time.

'Now, don't let Mamma intimidate you,' Daniel instructed. 'I have told her our situation and she has agreed to hear us out. I've had some ideas about how we could manage our lives. We'll talk this afternoon. But keep your head held high and treat this as just another social occasion.' She giggled.

'That's just what Nellie said. I'll have a very high head. Thank you very much for collecting me, Freddy.'

'No problem.'

'Are you staying for lunch?'

'Not this time. I'm certainly not going to intrude on such an important occasion. I'm sure Lady M isn't nearly as bad as she likes everyone to think. Good luck to the pair of you. I mean that, old boy. Lovely to meet you, Lizzie. I can see why he's head over heels for you.' He helped Daniel into his wheelchair and lifted Lizzie's case inside the door.

'Right, then. Here we go. Help me up the steps, will you, darling?'

Glad of something positive to do, Lizzie pushed him up the ramp which had been installed to one side of the steps. Her knees felt weak and she was already wondering what on earth was going to happen.

The hall seemed even larger without the massive Christmas tree. The marble floor echoed as they went across it. He asked if she wanted to tidy herself before lunch, but she said no. She took a deep breath as they went into the drawing room.

'Ah, Miss Vale. I hope you are well.'

'Lady Miles. I'm well, thank you. I hope the same of you.'

'Thank you.' She nodded. 'Will you

have a small sherry?'

'No, thank you,' Lizzie replied. 'A glass of water would be nice.' There was a man she took to be the butler in attendance and he poured water and a sherry and handed them out on a silver salver.

Lizzie sipped it gratefully. Rather stilted conversation filled the short gap before the lunch gong was sounded. She remembered the early days before the war at Cobridge House when a gong was sounded before each meal. Here, the formality seemed to overpower everything.

Daniel did his best to keep the conversation light but was met by a glare from his mother each time he said anything she didn't like. Lizzie hated the way she dominated her son but tried very hard not to let her feelings show. She was in a precarious enough position with this family and if she was to get what she and Daniel wanted, she needed to avoid any antagonism.

'I understand you actually work?' the woman said with such a tone of incredulity on her voice that Lizzie wanted to laugh.

'Yes. My brother-in-law is the owner of Cobridge China and my sister is their head designer. I am her personal assistant. She is currently confined at home after her new daughter's birth.'

'Extraordinary.' The look of disapproval was barely hidden.

'I noticed you have Cobridge china. This is actually one of my sister's designs.'

'Really? She has talent. It's a very pleasant range.' Lady Miles was clearly unimpressed. 'And you actually go to work at the factory, do you?'

'Well, yes. I do some work at home, when possible. While Nellie is at home, I bring mail for her to look at and keep everything moving in her department. It's all very busy but I enjoy it.'

'Lizzie writes as well. She publishes articles in the local press.'

'How bizarre. Goodness, I had no

idea that females were capable of such things.'

'Probably the ones you know would never be capable of any sort of work,' Daniel said in a tone that showed his irritation with his mother's attitude. 'I mean to say, arranging a few flowers and drinking tea seems all most of them are capable of doing.'

'Daniel, there's no need to be rude. What will Miss Vale think of you?'

Lizzie studied the pattern on her now-empty dinner plate, wishing this whole meal could be over as soon as possible. In fact, she was already regretting her decision to come at all. Then she looked at Daniel's dear face and knew exactly why she had come.

'Sorry, Mamma. Is Father coming back this afternoon?'

'I believe he will attend dinner this evening.' There was a pause which seemed to last for several minutes. She spoke again. 'I understand you still plan to go ahead with some sort of marriage?'

'Of course we do, Mamma,' Daniel said quickly. 'We plan a perfectly normal marriage.'

'I don't see how. But if you've found someone willing to take you on, who am I to complain about her.'

'I'd like to get an engagement ring for Lizzie. May we borrow the car and Alfred this afternoon?'

'Your father needs him. Do you really have to get a ring?'

'Of course. Unlike my brothers, I don't have access to a family heirloom to hand to my fiancée.'

'I won't have you visiting some common jeweller's shop in town. I believe there may be a ring available if you persist in this . . . ' She broke off.

Charade, Lizzie suspected she was about to say. She was feeling distinctly uncomfortable and was on the brink of telling this unmitigated snob she didn't want a ring. For Daniel's sake, she managed to bite her lip and keep her tongue in check.

'I think we may skip dessert, if that's

all right with you, Lizzie? I'd like to show her the grounds. We'll meet again at tea, no doubt.'

Gratefully, Lizzie began to fold her napkin but in time, noticed the protocol here seemed to be to leave it crumpled on the table. Obviously, a napkin was never used twice. She pushed the wheelchair round to Daniel and he got into it.

'Thank you for lunch,' Lizzie said politely. 'It was delicious.'

Lady Miles did not flicker any sort of reaction. They both breathed a sign of relief as they went outside.

'I'm so sorry. She can be the world's worst when something happens she doesn't like. I'm still being punished for defying her wishes and joining the air force. She was quite right, in that I stood a high chance of being injured. She doesn't know how to cope with it at all. Sees me as some sort of burden on her ordered life. One day she will come down to earth when she realises that the whole world has changed as a result of this war. She sees it as a slight inconvenience that she can't buy anything and everything she wants. She believes clothes coupons are vulgar and that she should have privileges because of her title.'

'She's a snob all right. But surely she should see that by marrying me, you are relieving her of the burden of having to look after you?'

'One of the things I was going to suggest is that we have an apartment here in the Hall. My little corner could easily be adapted for two of us and there's enough space to add a few more rooms to our allotted space.' Lizzie's face fell. She had been having similar ideas but at Cobridge House. 'But, I can see that it would never work. Mamma would expect us to dine with them and if that last little charade was anything to go by, it would never work.'

'We could live at Cobridge House. It's not that large but at least everyone would welcome us with love and caring.'

'I'm looking forward to meeting your family. Even if they do all have to work,' he added with a wicked grin.

They went along the well-tended pathways and gardens. Even at this time of year, everywhere looked immaculate. There were several flowering bushes to add colour and a few early snowdrops had poked their heads through the grass. It seemed there had been no need to dig up lawns to provide extra growing space for food as there was a massive kitchen garden. Greenhouses provided salad crops all through the year and she could see fruit trees trained across the warm walls of the whole area. Lizzie was entranced if not slightly overwhelmed by it all.

'I am assuming you would want to continue in your role working for Nellie, for a while longer at least.' She nodded. 'So living here isn't an option. It's much too far for you to travel each day. I don't feel I want to start our married life in your sister's house, however good to us they would be.'

'I suppose we could have one of the houses James has for his workers. There's probably one empty. He'd always make any modifications we need, I'm sure.'

They talked through several options but drew no conclusions. He could imagine how his mother would take the idea of her son living in a workman's house. But, as he acknowledged, he wanted to live his own life.

There was also the thorny problem of earning a living. His brothers had become involved in the family business and in managing the estate. They both had large self-contained apartments within the Hall and seemed to have lives apart from the dominance of Lady Miles. But then they had both toed the line and behaved exactly as she had wished.

'You're just a rebel, aren't you?' Lizzie said with a laugh. 'But we're no nearer solving anything. Maybe we're in for a long engagement.'

'I want us to be married as soon as

possible,' he said.

'I'd like that, too. But I don't see how. We need to work and we need a home. Apart from that, there are no problems.' They went inside for tea, bracing themselves for another encounter with Lady Miles. Lizzie went to the room she had been allocated and was pleased to see that she had risen in the ranks somewhat and was given a large, pretty room on the first floor. There was a bathroom attached so she felt rather luxurious.

Tea was more relaxed as Lady Miles did not put in an appearance. According to the maid, she was resting in her room and was to be served with a tray in there.

'I've already worn her out,' Lizzie said with a grin.

'I think she may be preparing for the evening. I'm afraid she has given the royal command to my brothers and wives and they are all to attend dinner tonight. I hope it won't be too much of an ordeal for you. Oh, perhaps I should have said, we always have to dress for dinner. I hope that won't be a problem?'

'No, I packed one of my best frocks. Mind you, I doubt that will cut it with her ladyship. Too common, don't you know. Oops, I'm sorry, Daniel.'

'Oh, Lizzie, I do love you. You are so wicked. You always manage to make me laugh. Just behave yourself this evening. You did meet the rest of the family at the New Years Eve party, so it won't be too dramatic.'

'Fingers crossed, eh?'

She drank the cocktail offered to her before dinner, thinking a small amount of alcohol might dispel her nerves a little. However much Daniel encouraged her, she could hardly fail to be anxious. His brothers were charming to her and their wives accepting, if not exactly enthusiastic. When the parents finally made their entrance, Lizzie was standing at one side, talking to the eldest son and swung round as the silence fell.

'Good evening, everyone,' Lady Miles boomed. They all murmured their responses. Sir Geoffrey, as she quickly learned his name to be, came over and spoke to her.

'I don't believe we've met. You intend to marry my son, I gather?' He seemed a little more human than his wife and smiled in a friendly manner as he held out his hand.

'I hope so, sir. My name is Lizzie. Lizzie Vale. I suppose I'm really Elizabeth, but I have never been called that.' She stopped suddenly, her inner voice telling her to stop prattling.

'I hope I may call you Lizzie, then.'

'Of course, Sir Geoffrey. I'd be delighted.'

'Very good. Very good,' he said, moving away duty done.

'Don't look so scared, love,' Daniel told her. 'He liked you, I can tell. He's much less of a snob than my mother. I'll tell you about her own background one of these days. I'm sure that's why she seems such a snob. But not now, we still have this meal to get through. You'll be sitting opposite to me this time. I think you are to sit between my brothers.'

'What do I call them?'

'I'd suggest Abbott and Costello but their names are Thomas and Matthew.'

Lizzie giggled and tried to keep her face straight as they were called in to the meal.

'Which one is Abbott?' she whispered.

The dinner was a surprisingly pleasant occasion. Lady Miles barely spoke to Lizzie, but as there was plenty of conversation, she felt much more at ease. Thomas and Matthew were relentless in questioning her about their plans.

'You may have to push this blighter to make a decent woman of you before you're fifty,' Thomas, the elder brother said.

'We plan to marry as soon as things can be settled.'

'Jolly good show. He's a lucky chap

to find someone like you.'

'Thank you,' Lizzie said gratefully. At least someone approved of her.

Towards the end of the meal Sir Geoffrey stood and clinked a glass to call for attention.

'I felt it appropriate to say a few words. As you all know, we have with us Elizabeth, Lizzie, who it seems is to join our family at some point in the future. I'd like us all to raise our glasses to Lizzie and Daniel and to welcome her to the family.' They all stood and raised their glasses.

'To Lizzie and Daniel,' everyone said. She blushed and smiled across the table at the man she loved. She sneaked a glance at Lady Miles, sitting at the opposite end of the table. Though she raised her glass, she did not join in the toast.

'Now, I understand that they wish to marry as soon as it can be arranged,' Sir Geoffrey continued. 'We are all aware of the difficulties the recent war inflicted on Daniel and so I propose to assist in whatever way I can. I am proposing to gift one of our houses to him. To them. There will have to be some work done to make it suitable. I am also proposing to bestow a regular allowance on him. We all owe a debt of gratitude on him and his fellow officers for their efforts to save our country. Thank you.'

There was a long silence following this speech. Lizzie could have said nothing, even if asked. She was totally overwhelmed at the unexpected announcement.

She looked up as Daniel rose to his feet. Supporting himself on the table, he spoke.

'Thank you, Father. I am sure we are both very grateful for your offer. I hope to be able to carry out some sort of proper work in the future, but at present many tasks seem insurmountable for me. But as you can see, I am improving each week and with Lizzie's help I intend to become entirely mobile again, one day. We hope to marry as soon as possible. I love you, Lizzie, with all my heart and I am grateful to you for agreeing to be my wife.'

Lizzie blushed once more and felt tears filling her eyes in a ridiculously embarrassing way. Thomas took her hand and squeezed it comfortingly.

'Welcome to this crazy family,' he whispered.

Family Love

Although Lady Miles continued to keep herself apart from the family celebrations, the weekend passed swiftly and very pleasantly.

On Sunday evening, Alfred was appointed to drive her back, accompanied by Daniel. They sat together in the rear of the car. He took her hand and gave her a ring. It was a single ruby, set in a circle of tiny diamonds.

'I think it belonged to my grandmother. My father has given it to us. If you'd prefer something else, you only have to say and we can go and choose something you like better.'

'It's beautiful. Really beautiful. Thank you, Daniel and thank you to your father. I like him. He seems a very generous man.'

'And he makes up for my mother?'

'I never said that.'

'You don't need to. But once we've agreed on this house he's offering, let's make our plans to be married.'

'Yes, please.'

'They'll probably want us to be married from the Hall. Can you cope with that?'

'I suppose so. I'd rather it was a small affair, though. My family really don't do big weddings.'

'I'll see what I can do. Can't promise anything. You know Mamma.'

'Not really. What were you going to tell me about her background?' She whispered in a low voice, so Alfred couldn't hear.

'Well, she was actually the daughter of one of the Brown's Pottery family.'

'Brown's? But they were one of James's main rivals. Guilty of industrial espionage at one time. They copied some of his designs and produced them in heavy earthenware. I think Brown went bankrupt during the early part of the war.'

'Quite correct. So her pedigree isn't

that much to write home about. They married despite my grandfather's objections. I think once she had her claws into my father, there was no going back. I must say, I hope she's nicer to him in private than she is in public.'

'Goodness me. I think I'm less afraid of her now you've told me that.'

She persuaded Daniel to come in and meet her family briefly. Lizzie immediately burst out with the news of Sir Geoffrey's offer.

'I can't believe she has never introduced you to us before now,' Nellie told Daniel. 'It's lovely to know that things seem to be working out for you. James and I will do anything we can to help, of course.'

'Thank you. I look forward to getting to know you all much better, though I feel as if I know you already after everything Lizzie has told me. You seem like a wonderfully close family. I look forward to being a part of it very soon. Now, I should return home or my father will be thinking I've stolen his car and driver.'

Lizzie stood on the doorstep to wave him goodbye. She hugged her arms round her body, her smile fixed firmly into place. She was marrying the man she loved. They would have a home and an income. How could she not smile? Life was about to get more wonderful than she could ever have believed.

The next few weeks seemed to fly by in a flurry of wedding preparations, furnishing the house that Sir Geoffrey had assigned to them. It was a large house, near to one of the parks and within reach of the Cobridge factory, in case Lizzie wanted to stay on.

It had been owned by one of the family relatives and had lain empty since before the war. It had been entirely re-fitted, with several extras added to make Daniel's life easier. There was even a lift installed so that he could get upstairs without difficulty.

'I can't believe how kind he's being,' Lizzie told her sister. 'When I think I nearly walked out when Lady M was so horrid to me. And the best of it is that she is no posher than I am. She just likes to give the impression that she is so very much better than the rest of us.' She laughed. 'I can't wait to see her face when our lot turn up in force at the wedding. Joe and Daisy are never ones to put on airs and I suspect Ben and Jenny will be their lovely practical selves.'

'And I suppose you have no fears about James and me disgracing ourselves?'

'Course not. He's posh enough for both of you. But, I'm sorry the wedding won't be here. I've asked for just a small affair but she's probably got a guest list nine miles long. Let's hope they can't all come.'

The day before the wedding, Lizzie's whole family arrived to stay overnight at Dalmere Hall, ready for the ceremony. There was a small church on the estate which was filled to bursting.

Daniel had insisted that he was going to stand for the ceremony and wanted to walk down the aisle with his new wife. No way would he accept that the wheelchair would be used. He turned to look for his bride, as the organ played the wedding march and assisted by his friend, Freddie, stood as she reached the altar.

'You look beautiful,' he whispered. Somehow, some silk had been found and a simple, straight dress was created to show off her slim figure perfectly. Her one concession to Lady Miles, when she refused a family wedding dress, was to accept a lace veil and a simple diamond tiara, used by all the brides in recent years.

After the ceremony, Daniel managed to walk up the aisle as planned.

'I'm so proud of you, darling,' she whispered.

'So am I. But I need to sit down now. Getting married to you is an exhausting business.'

He kissed her, while still standing. There was applause from them all.

'To our future, together,' Lizzie said happily.

Books by Chrissie Loveday
in the Linford Romance Library:

WHERE THE HEART IS
OUT OF THE BLUE
TOMORROW'S DREAMS
DARE TO LOVE
WHERE LOVE BELONGS

We do hope that you have enjoyed reading this large print book.

Did you know that all of our titles are available for purchase?

We publish a wide range of high quality large print books including:
Romances, Mysteries, Classics
General Fiction
Non Fiction and Westerns

Special interest titles available in large print are:
The Little Oxford Dictionary
Music Book, Song Book
Hymn Book, Service Book

Also available from us courtesy of Oxford University Press:
Young Readers' Dictionary
(large print edition)
Young Readers' Thesaurus
(large print edition)

For further information or a free brochure, please contact us at:
Ulverscroft Large Print Books Ltd.,
The Green, Bradgate Road, Anstey,
Leicester, LE7 7FU, England.
Tel: (00 44) **0116 236 4325**
Fax: (00 44) **0116 234 0205**

THE GIRL FROM YESTERDAY

Teresa Ashby

Robert Ashton and Kate Gibson are a month away from their wedding. However, Robert's ex-wife Caroline turns up from Australia with a teen-age daughter, Karen, who Robert knew nothing about. Then, as Caroline and Robert spend time together, they still seem to have feelings for one another, despite the fact that Jim, back in Australia, has asked Caroline to marry him. Now, Robert and Caroline must decide whether their futures lie with each other — or with Kate and Jim.

LOVERS NEVER LIE

Gael Morrison

Stacia Roberts has always played it safe, yet, longing for adventure, she travels to Greece expecting sunshine and excitement — and gets more than she'd ever bargained for. When strangers try to kill her, she suspects her fellow traveller Andrew Moore might be the enemy — but is he really a friend? Andrew blames himself for his wife's death. Then he falls in love with Stacia, vowing to keep her safe, a difficult task when he discovers she's an international thief.